Annie's
Mysteries Unraveled™

Finished Off

Jan Fields

Annie's®
AnniesFiction.com

Finished Off
Copyright © 2015 Annie's.

The characters and events in this book are fictional, and any resemblance to actual persons or events is coincidental.

Library of Congress-in-Publication Data
Finished Off / by Jan Fields
p. cm.
I. Title
                    2015946723

AnniesFiction.com
(800) 282-6643
Annie's Mysteries Unraveled™
Series Creators: Janice Tate and Ken Tate
Series Editors: Shari Lohner, Janice Tate, and Ken Tate
Cover Illustrator: Kelley McMorris

10 11 12 13 14 | Printed in China | 9 8 7 6 5 4 3 2 1

One

The restaurant at the Hamilton Arms hotel in downtown Fort Worth had gently curved walls, one of which was made up almost entirely of tall windows. Despite the heat of the Texas summer outside, the restaurant was chilly enough to make Kate Stevens glad she'd worn a light jacket. The restaurant patrons seated at small, glass-topped tables near the windows enjoyed the view of colorful planting beds that surrounded the hotel.

At one of these tables, Vivi Lawrence leaned forward, perched on the edge of her chair with her legs crossed neatly at the ankle, her hands wrapped around a mug of mocha latte. "Work was crazy this morning, and I have plenty more waiting for me when we're done. It seems like Fridays are always like that lately," she said as she tucked a strand of blond hair behind her ear. "Anyway, I'm sorry we had to have lunch at the hotel."

The concern in her friend's voice registered in Kate's distracted attention. She smiled apologetically and smoothed the napkin in her lap nervously. "The hotel restaurant is wonderful as always. And really, I'm glad to be able to spend any time with you at all."

"You could have fooled me." Vivi gave her a wry smile followed by a pretend pout. "I'm not sure you even heard the last three things I said about Sam."

Kate felt a pang of guilt. Vivi was Kate's best friend and definitely deserved better than Kate's distracted fog.

She hadn't even realized the conversation had drifted to Sam Tennyson, the handsome Texas Ranger Vivi had been dating on and off for months. Kate liked the tall, serious man and thought Vivi was probably good for him. She made Sam laugh, and Kate suspected he didn't do a lot of that otherwise.

Kate fidgeted with the fork beside her plate. "I'm sorry. I can't seem to shake off the gloomies."

"Because of the argument with Vanessa?" Vivi asked gently.

Kate nodded, surprised to find herself fighting tears. She hated arguing with her daughter. Of course, raising a strong-willed, independent daughter like Vanessa had its challenges, but serious arguments were still rare. Mostly Kate felt like she and her daughter were a team, but she didn't like the way a certain young actor popped up again and again in Vanessa's conversations lately. If she were honest with herself, Kate would acknowledge that she had always worried about Vanessa's friendship with Logan Lariby, even when they had lived in Stony Point, Maine.

"Do you really think this boy is bad for her?" Vivi asked. "I know young people in Hollywood can get involved in some pretty terrible things."

Kate shook her head, sending her straight dark hair swinging around her face. "No, he's not like that. I'm sure of that much. Vanessa has known Logan for years, ever since he was part of a movie shot back in Stony Point. He's a nice guy, and I certainly don't blame Vanessa for liking him. But I think he'd like to be more than friends, and I'd hate to see Vanessa's schooling get sidetracked. She's smart and determined and talented. She could do anything with her life. As much as I like Logan, I don't want him to become her life."

"Vanessa isn't you, you know."

No matter how gently it was spoken, that stung. Kate had married Vanessa's father right out of high school. She'd never gotten to go to college, and she had really struggled when her marriage fell apart. She corrected that thought, refusing to lie to herself after all these years. The reality was that her marriage had never really held together in the first place. Harry was a sweet guy when he was sober, but those moments had grown fewer and fewer as the years passed. Eventually, she found herself with little education, a teenage daughter to raise, and the self-esteem of a wet noodle. If it hadn't been for her crocheting and her kind friends in Stony Point, she didn't know how they would have gotten through those years. Kate didn't want that for Vanessa.

"I probably overreacted," Kate said, straightening in her chair.

"Probably?"

Kate smiled slightly. "Right. I definitely overreacted." Then she groaned. "You know my mom didn't like Harry, which made him all the more appealing. What if *I'm* the one who makes Vanessa do something stupid like run away with an actor?"

"Vanessa has a good head on her shoulders, and she's pretty driven to find a place for herself in this world. I don't think she's going to rush off with this young man because you disapprove," Vivi said, her eyes twinkling as her smile turned mischievous, "even if he is more adorable in person than in his movies."

"Thanks. That makes me feel a lot better."

Vivi laughed. "Have you tried calling her and groveling for forgiveness?"

Kate nodded. "She's not answering her phone. Actually,

she's probably just not answering *my* calls." She slumped slightly in her chair. "Sometimes being the mother of a young woman is far more stressful than being the mother of a toddler."

"I wouldn't know about either," Vivi said with a sigh. "Most of our clients are businesspeople here at the hotel, but we do get the occasional young family. There's nothing like a really cute baby to make you wish you had one."

"Oh, and how about the screaming babies?"

Vivi laughed. "They do make it a little easier to be single."

Kate's smile faded. "I wish I could patch things up with my baby."

Vivi leaned back in her chair and sipped at her mocha latte. "You can always talk it out when she gets home."

"Which won't be until almost the end of summer. I've been sending text messages, but you really can't talk much through that. Vanessa did agree to a video chat after church on Sunday. I guess I'll save my apology until then, unless she decides to call me back."

"Well," Vivi said, "I imagine the archaeological dig is keeping her pretty busy, especially as the undergraduate gofer. She might not be spending as much time fretting about this as you are."

"Probably not. But I'm the mom; fretting is my superpower."

Vivi took another sip of her mocha latte, and her eyes sparkled. "Then you could fret about the heat and the hard work and the mosquitoes and the bears."

Kate's eyes widened. "There are bears in Texas?"

"See? I gave you something new to worry about besides the fight."

"Wow. Thanks, pal," Kate said. "Now tell me, are there really bears?"

"I've never seen one."

"Well, I can't imagine they're checking into hotels," Kate said. She wondered if Vanessa was taking proper precautions about bears. From what she'd seen on nature shows, Kate was fairly sure you were supposed to put your food in trees. *Will Vanessa know to keep her food out of reach?*

"I've been camping," Vivi said, pulling Kate's attention back to her. "I've never seen a bear."

"You've been camping?"

"I don't spend *all* my time working. I have fun. Which reminds me, I wanted to ask you something."

Kate snatched her phone out of her neat crocheted purse and pulled up Vanessa's contact info. "One second. I want to send Vanessa a quick message about this bear thing."

Vivi put her hand on Kate's arm. "Honestly, I don't think you have to worry about bears. I shouldn't have brought it up. Vanessa is more likely to be worked to death than anything else. Anytime you're the gofer, you keep pretty busy."

"At least she's splitting the job with her roommate Maddie." Kate reluctantly dropped her phone back into her purse and returned to pushing her salad around with her fork. "This archaeological dig is another thing I don't quite understand. Vanessa has never shown any interest in archaeology, and now she's off on a dig near the Brazos River."

Vivi grinned. "But an archaeological dig sounds so cool and romantic."

"You're kidding," Kate said. "It sounds sweaty and dirty to me, and then there's the whole bear issue."

"You have no sense of adventure," Vivi scolded. "I was a business major, and I would have jumped at a chance to do something like that. I'm amazed she was even invited."

"It's because of Maddie. She's an anthropology major, and Vanessa met the professor who's overseeing the dig through her. Apparently the professor is brilliant. She has doctorates in both archaeology and anthropology. Vanessa couldn't talk about her enough and her theories about aggression and population growth." Kate wrinkled her nose. "I don't find the idea of spending the summer in the dust and heat at all appealing."

"Unearthing *history*. Haven't you ever heard of Indiana Jones?"

Kate laughed. "I doubt they're going to run across treasure or ancient ruins. Vanessa said they're mostly expecting to find broken pottery and maybe some arrowheads."

"Don't rain on my adventure fantasies."

"Never." Kate took a bite of the salad she'd been halfheartedly poking at. It was delicious, with perfectly grilled chicken and tangy dried cranberries. "This is really good."

Vivi's face lit up. "It's about time you ate some of it. I was starting to feel guilty for wolfing mine down. It's my favorite thing they serve here, so I've eaten a lot of salad."

"Which explains your figure," Kate said. "I should choose salad a little more often."

"I know a certain police detective who seems to like the way you look exactly as you are."

As she felt the warmth flood her cheeks, Kate took another bite of salad to hide her embarrassment. After her divorce, she would have been perfectly content to fly solo for the rest of her life. Peter Matthews had come as a disconcerting surprise. Though she loved the time she spent with Peter, she still blushed at references to his obvious affection for her.

"Since it's possible you didn't hear anything I said about

Sam," Vivi said, her impish smile making it plain she wasn't mad about Kate's distracted mood, "I'll repeat myself a smidge and ask the question your bear panic derailed."

"Yes, sorry about that," Kate said. "Ask away."

"Sam asked me to go camping in Stonewall County later in the month if he can wrap up the case he's on. I have some time off, and we thought we'd spend it together. I wondered if you and Peter might like to come along. I have a big tent that you and I can share, and you'd be amazed at how comfortable those inflatable mattresses can be."

"Camping?" Kate echoed. "I think you missed my views on being out in the hot Texas sun, not to mention the woods that are apparently filled with bears."

"You went horseback riding with me in the hot Texas sun."

"And look at how that turned out."

"You can't blame that on nature," Vivi scolded. "You could meet bad guys anywhere." She lowered her voice and looked around theatrically. "There could even be some in here."

Kate crossed her arms. "At least there aren't any bears in here."

"You really need to forget about bears. I mean, we'll be with a pair of hunky law enforcement types."

"That's true," Kate said, imagining Peter in hiking boots and toting a backpack.

"Also, the heat won't be so bad next to the river, and we'll be in Stonewall County. Isn't that where Vanessa's dig is?"

Kate nodded in response as she took a bite of her salad.

"Maybe we could 'accidentally' run into them. Do you know the town closest to the dig site?"

"That I do know," Kate said. She pulled her phone from her purse and flipped through her messages. "The name of the town is Elijahville. Vanessa described it as built from cinder block and dust."

"Sounds charming. I guess we *could* happen to camp near there," Vivi suggested, though with less than her usual enthusiasm.

"I don't know if that would be a good idea. Vanessa thinks I don't trust her to make her own decisions. That's part of why she's mad at me. I'm not sure showing up at her summer job would exactly smooth things over."

Vivi shrugged. "Well, keep it in mind. And we could always camp somewhere prettier, if you want. You should mention it to Peter."

"Not likely. Peter would *love* the idea of a camping trip, especially since he gets along so well with Sam. I'm the one who likes to tuck into my own bed at night, and I like a nice sturdy building around me when I sleep. The great outdoors is for day trips only. Plus, if I can get Vanessa to agree to weekly computer chats, I'm definitely not going to be out in the wilderness and miss one."

"Right. That doesn't sound like a mother hen at all."

Kate made a face at her friend, receiving a laugh in return. The phone in her hand burst into song, and her face lit up when she saw the name on the screen. "Excuse me. It's Vanessa."

"Of course," Vivi said, her face reflecting the happy surprise on Kate's.

Kate held the phone up to her ear. "Sweetheart, I'm so glad you called."

On the other end of the phone, Kate heard a soft shuffling sound and then a single hushed word. "Mom?" She recognized Vanessa's voice in the shaky whisper.

"Vanessa? Is something wrong—" The call ended before

Kate could finish the question, leaving her to stare in alarm at her silent phone.

Two

As she stared at the phone in her hand, Kate was only vaguely aware of Vivi calling her name. She pulled up Vanessa on her contact list and tried to call, but only got the voice mail. She tried again with the same result.

Vivi reached across the table and touched Kate's arm. "Kate, what's wrong?"

"I don't know," Kate said. "We were cut off."

"What did Vanessa say?" Vivi asked.

"'Mom.'" Kate decided to punch in the number directly. Logically, she knew that wouldn't make any difference, but being logical wasn't her main concern at the moment. Again her call rolled to voice mail. "She was almost whispering. Why would she call me when she couldn't talk unless it was important?"

"Maybe she was calling from a public restroom," Vivi said. "I always whisper when I have to make a call in the restroom. Or maybe she has a cold. It doesn't have to be something terrible."

"It sounded terrible," Kate said, trying the number again.

"Are you sure you're not reading too much into it?" Vivi asked. "You were already worried about Vanessa. Maybe you're letting your imagination run away with you a little."

Kate wanted to defend her worry, but she knew Vivi could be right. "Of course." She stopped and looked up at her friend as she passed her phone nervously from one hand to the other. "I wish I could talk to her."

"Well, Vanessa knows you, so I'm sure she'll call again as soon as she can get a signal. If she's out in the boondocks, it might be hard to get a call through, especially when you're redialing constantly."

Kate stopped in the middle of punching in the number again and placed the phone very pointedly on the table next to her plate. She forced a smile. "You're right. I'll crank back the worry and give her a chance to call back." She forced herself to take another bite of her salad, though she suspected she looked about as relaxed and casual as a cat in a dog park.

Vivi watched Kate for a moment and then checked her watch and groaned. "I have to get back to work. Are you going to be all right?"

Kate nodded. "I'm fine. You've talked me down off the ledge. I'll head home and wait for Vanessa to call back."

"OK," Vivi said, standing up slowly. "Don't worry about lunch, it's on my tab. And if the phone rings while you're in the car, pull off the road to answer. Vanessa doesn't need you getting into a car wreck from talking on the cell and driving."

"Now who's being a mother hen?" Kate asked.

"Make that a best-friend hen. Cluck-cluck."

"I'll see you later, chickie," Kate said. She picked up her phone, slipped it into her purse, and stood to give Vivi a quick hug goodbye.

On the drive back to Sage Hills, Kate was constantly alert for spots to pull off the road in case her cell rang. She'd placed the phone on the console next to her so she wouldn't have to fumble in her purse for it. For all her preparations, the phone stayed stubbornly silent throughout the drive.

Once home, she wandered from room to room, carrying the phone with her. She finally decided that she needed to do something to distract herself instead of letting her worry build until her head blew up.

She gratefully turned to work. It wasn't the first time that crochet had provided a welcome distraction. She needed to finish some edging on a new crocheted children's jacket for her latest book of designs for Brighton & Craig Publishing. Each design was inspired by a different children's book. The sturdy little blue–and–yellow jacket would have been right at home on Heidi as she tagged along behind the goatherd in the Alps. She'd spoken with her editor, Alexus, earlier in the week and knew that finishing this last project early would make everyone happy.

She'd decided on a complicated edging to give the jacket a modern twist. She hoped working on the intricate pattern would help keep her mind distracted. Gathering the fine yarn and jacket from her design studio, she carried them to her front room and settled into the comfy Queen Anne chair that had become her favorite place to crochet. It was exactly the right distance from the front windows, letting her work in natural light.

As always, crocheting had an almost magical effect on Kate's nerves. As the soft yellow yarn slipped through her fingers, her thoughts turned toward listing logical reasons why Vanessa might whisper into the phone. She was on a dig with a bunch of other young people. Maybe she was a little embarrassed to be calling her mother.

She thought of the times when Vanessa had been a high school girl, chatting on the phone with her friends, her voice almost a whisper so Kate wouldn't hear which boys Vanessa and her friends liked. The memory brought a slight smile to Kate's lips. She had overreacted because of their fight. All she had to do was wait for Vanessa to call back, which was certain to be soon. Still, she snuck more than one glance at the cellphone lying on the small table beside her.

Kate discovered the edging she'd planned for the jacket didn't look as good as she'd hoped. It was too bulky, and it distracted from the jacket's neat lines. With a sigh, she pulled out the careful rows of stitching, winding them back onto the yarn ball. Then she started a new stitch and was soon so caught up that she barely noticed the passage of time. At one point she was vaguely aware that her light was fading, but she didn't recall switching on the lamp.

When she heard a knock on the door, Kate checked the time on her phone and found it was later than she'd thought. It was probably Vivi stopping on her way home from work to make sure Kate wasn't still upset.

She fought down a fresh pang of worry. What had kept Vanessa from calling back? She slipped the phone into the pocket of her light cotton pants and called out to Vivi before she fully opened the door, "I'm fine."

"I've always thought so." Peter Matthews offered her the crooked grin that tended to make her stomach flutter. Not that she'd tell him that. He leaned against the doorframe, looking good in his short-sleeved denim shirt, jeans, and ever-present cowboy boots. As always, his thick, dark hair looked like he'd been running his fingers through it, sending it into wild disarray.

"Oh, hi," Kate said. "I thought you were Vivi."

Peter laughed. "Now that's an unusual case of mistaken identity, considering I'm nearly a foot taller than she is."

"Otherwise, you're a dead ringer." Kate stepped back to let Peter in.

"I get that all the time," Peter said, playing along.

"You two do have things in common. She teases me mercilessly too."

"And does she do this?" He leaned over and kissed her lightly.

"No, definitely not." She felt her cheeks warm, and she spoke quickly to head off the teasing she knew she'd get about her blush. "This is a nice surprise."

"It's not supposed to be," Peter said, frowning slightly. "We actually had a date scheduled for tonight."

Kate's eyes widened. "Oh, right. I'm so sorry. I totally forgot."

"You're absolutely horrible for my ego. Did you know that?" He glanced at the chair. "Was it the crocheting? I guess I can forgive you for getting wrapped up in your work."

Kate looked toward the chair and considered agreeing with him to avoid another scolding about overreacting. Finally, she sighed. "Not really. I was crocheting, but mostly I forgot because of Vanessa."

"You're still upset about the fight? You know, she's probably forgiven you by now. She doesn't seem like the type to hold a grudge. She's too much like her mother for that."

"You're right," Kate said. Vanessa wasn't the sort to hold on to such things, and she usually forgot them faster even than Kate did. "Actually, she did try to call, but we were cut off, which isn't helping my nerves."

Peter watched Kate's face carefully. "Well, she is working pretty far out. She probably couldn't get a good signal."

"I know, but the call was so strange. Vanessa was whispering. And she didn't speak right away. Then all she managed to say was 'Mom' before we were cut off."

"Did you try to call her back?" Peter held up his hand as Kate opened her mouth. "Forget that question; of course you tried to call her back. I take it you couldn't get through."

Kate shook her head.

"Again, it could be the location, especially if Vanessa called from the dig site. I've been in that area, and reception can be spotty. She might have to wait to call when she's closer to town."

"Maybe," Kate said. She knew Peter was being completely reasonable, but somehow she couldn't let go of her worry. She glanced down at her clothes and smoothed the wrinkles in her slacks. "I really should change before we go out."

"You look fine," he said.

She looked up at him. "I believe that's what my mother used to call 'damning with faint praise.'"

"In that case, you look fantastic."

"Now you're being silly."

"But you're not laughing." He gave her a hug.

Kate hadn't realized how tense her shoulders were until Peter put his arms around them.

"Although I'm completely certain that Vanessa's fine, we could head up there in the morning and see for ourselves."

"We could?"

He shrugged one shoulder. "Why not? I'm off work this weekend, and I'm really ready to get away from the city for a couple of days."

"A couple of *days*?"

Peter grinned. "We can make a weekend of it. I know a friend who has a cabin near the river. He's let me use it before for fishing. I love the Brazos River area. It'll be fun."

Kate stared at him for a moment. This was the second effort made in one day to get her to Stonewall County. She wondered if it could be a sign. Her mother had also often talked about the Lord working in mysterious ways.

"I don't even know exactly where the dig site is," Kate said.

Peter frowned. "Do you know the nearest town?"

"Elijahville. Vanessa mentioned that's where they get supplies and snacks."

"As fate would have it, Elijahville is close to my friend's cabin. We should go for the weekend."

Kate frowned. "I don't believe in fate."

"Not a problem," Peter said. "The cabin will be there anyway, and we can easily drive into town to chat up the locals. In a small town, an archaeological dig would be big news. Someone will know where it is."

When Kate didn't respond, Peter continued with his pitch.

"It's a nice cabin, though maybe a little rustic. But there's plenty of room for you to have all the privacy you need. Mostly I want you to get things settled with Vanessa so you don't forget any more dates. My ego can only take so much." He put a hand to his chest.

Despite his teasing tone, Kate couldn't miss the hope in his eyes. Peter loved the outdoors, but Texas summers were still taking a little getting used to for Kate. This was her third since moving to Texas, and the mild winter and spring of the past few months had lulled her into a false sense of security about the brutally hot months of summer. Kate still preferred the almost constant breezes off the water back in Maine. She rubbed her hands together nervously as she tried to organize the conflicting thoughts in her head.

"If we don't find Vanessa tomorrow, we might have to come back here. She's supposed to connect with me by computer on Sunday, and I don't want to risk missing that."

"We could always find someone with Wi-Fi on Sunday," Peter suggested. "It's the countryside, not the frontier."

"Is the cabin safe from bears?" Kate asked.

Peter's hopeful look turned bewildered. "Bears? I don't think you have to worry about bears. I've never seen a bear down there. We might see some coyotes."

"Do they bite?"

Peter ran his hand through his hair, clearly confused by the strange turn the conversation had taken. "We're not going to try to pet them, Kate. They're wild animals; they don't want to be involved with people. Honestly, you'd have a much greater chance of running into a snake or scorpion."

"Snakes?" Kate's eyes widened in horror. "Scorpions? Are you trying to make me feel better about this trip?"

"Think of it as another new adventure, like horseback riding. You liked that."

"In a terrifying way," she agreed.

"Some of the best things in life are scary," Peter said. He held up his cellphone. "Do you want me to call my friend and ask about the cabin?"

Kate thought of the tension she'd heard when Vanessa whispered into the phone. What if Vanessa had run into a snake or scorpions or something even worse? With a shudder, she made her decision. "Yes, let's go find my daughter."

Three

The morning sun poured through the windows and created squares of light on the quilt that covered Kate's bed. She felt the warmth of the sun that would turn to melting heat once she got out in it. Still, she was glad they were going to do something. After a night of poor rest, she felt like she might climb out of her skin if they didn't get moving.

She'd gotten up early and had drunk enough coffee to feel slightly twitchy. Then she stressed over what to pack into the small duffel bag on her bed. She wasn't entirely sure what one took camping. How could she know what the cabin already had? Maybe she should pack bed linens. There was no telling what level of cleanliness guys on a fishing trip thought was acceptable, and she doubted the cabin had a washer and dryer after Peter had described it as "rustic."

She added sheets to the duffel bag, choosing the plain blue ones over the dainty pink floral in an effort to be a little bit more rustic. She stared into her luggage and wondered if there was room to cram in her pillow. There was.

"Disinfectant," she muttered. "I should bring disinfectant." She went in search of a can. After a full night with no message from Vanessa, Kate was beyond worry. Vanessa would have realized her call would scare her mother. *Something* was wrong.

The phone rang as Kate was shoving cans of disinfectant into her bulging bag. Since she'd been carrying her cell everywhere, even sleeping with it next to her pillow, she answered Vivi's call within seconds.

"Have you heard from Vanessa?" Vivi asked.

"No, but I'm heading to Elijahville today."

"Alone?" Vivi yelped. "I couldn't possibly get a camping trip organized that quick. I don't think Sam's done with the case he's working."

"No camping. I'm going with Peter. It was actually his idea. I have to make sure Vanessa is all right, even if she ends up furious with me. It's not like her to leave me worried like this."

"I understand. If you need anything from me, you'll let me know, right?"

"Of course," Kate agreed. "I do have a question."

"What's that?"

"Can you kill scorpions with bug spray?"

"Where did you hear about scorpions?" Vivi asked. "I'm never going to get you out camping, am I?"

"Peter told me about the scorpions and the snakes, so the answer is no. I'm not interested in recreation that features either of those things. This trip is strictly to find Vanessa and make sure she's OK." Kate paused. "Oh, and to give her some bug spray, because I'm certain she didn't know about the scorpions."

"Maybe she didn't want to worry you."

"Well, that's working well," Kate said, then stopped and took a deep breath. She didn't want to take her worry out on Vivi. "I'm sorry for being snappy."

"That's all right," Vivi said. "That's one of the things friends are for—venting. Now be sure to keep me updated on Vanessa."

"I will. Um, there's one other thing," Kate said.

"Sure, what do you need?" Vivi asked, her cheerful voice making it clear she wasn't at all annoyed with Kate's crabbiness.

"This cabin is apparently out in the woods. I got the GPS coordinates from Peter, and I want to give them to you. You know, in case I disappear."

"I don't think Peter's going to let you disappear," Vivi said.

"I know," Kate agreed. "But, you know, in case we're attacked by bears or something."

Vivi hooted with laughter. "Kate, I'm sorry. Really. You don't have to worry about bears."

"Sure, but let me give you the coordinates anyway." She pulled the slip of paper from her pocket and read the numbers out to Vivi. Her friend dutifully read them back.

"But really, do try to have fun," Vivi suggested.

"I will," Kate said. "Right after I talk to Vanessa."

After she hung up, Kate stuffed two cans of bug spray into her duffel alongside the disinfectant. She had to pull the gap closed with one hand and zip it up with the other. Fortunately, the bag had a heavy-duty zipper. She hauled it off the bed, staggered into the front room, and dropped it beside the front door. Maybe Peter would carry it out to the truck for her.

She paced while she waited for him, running Vanessa's brief phone call over and over in her head. It was like having a bit of frayed yarn in a sweater. She couldn't leave it alone, and she picked at the memory over and over.

When she opened the door, Peter took one look at her and engulfed her in a hug. "It's going to be all right," he said, his voice making his chest rumble against Kate's ear. "We'll find Vanessa. I promise."

"Be careful about promises."

"I'm always careful about promises, and I plan to keep this one. Now, are you ready to go?"

Kate stepped away from him and nodded.

"Is this your only bag?" Peter reached down to snag the duffel with one hand, then groaned. "What did you pack in here—Vivi?"

"No, just the things I thought I might need."

"You do remember that we're only going for the weekend."

"I like being prepared."

He gave her a smile. "That's my Girl Scout. Let's get this thing out to the truck. I hope my suspension can handle the weight."

"Funny," Kate grumbled as she followed him out the door.

Peter kept up cheerful patter for most of the ride, telling her funny stories about the guys he worked with. Kate tried to pay attention, but her mind wandered as she twisted her fingers together in her lap.

"You're going to end up with sore joints if you keep that up, and then who'll finish your book?" Peter reached over and put his hand on hers.

His touch helped Kate relax a bit. She glanced out the window at the countryside. The land was nothing like rural Maine. They seemed to pass mile after mile of fields where the primary ground cover was grass, both faded green and summer-baked brown. Heat shimmered on the road ahead. Now and again they would come to long stretches of fencing where cows stood in burnt grass and stared at them as they passed.

"Sometimes I feel like I've moved to a totally different planet," Kate said.

Peter cut a sideways glance at her. "I've never been to Maine. How is it different? I mean, in the rural areas like this?"

"Lots more trees," Kate said. "And you'll see these piled-stone walls through the trees where the original settlers moved stones out of the potential farmland and stacked them up to make low walls that wind through the woods near the roads."

"Sounds pretty."

"It is," Kate said. "The trees grow right up close to the edge of the old, windy roads. In towns, the buildings are often close together. They were built narrow and tall—three stories aren't unusual."

"Did you live in one of those tall houses?" Peter asked.

Kate shook her head. "No, my house wasn't all that different from the one I have now. I guess I always tend to roost in the same kinds of nests."

"I'm glad you flew south." Peter gave her hand a squeeze. "We'll be in Elijahville soon."

"Really?" Kate looked in all directions but saw no sign of an approaching town. When they had passed inhabited land, it usually held old mobile homes, including some dull silver trailers that Kate had never seen outside of movies. Other buildings looked scoured and tired. "Where's the river?"

"We're closer than you think, and we'll see a lot more trees when we drive up to the cabin," Peter answered. "The woods extended farther from the river until settlers came and started farms. A lot of these roads were built so farmers could carry crops and livestock to market, and they still don't see much traffic."

They passed a bent sign announcing Elijahville. Kate was grateful for the sign because there was nothing about the surroundings that said "town." Down the road a bit they passed single-story houses with tiny brown lawns, some strewn with toys. Between them, the occasional business popped up, many related to farming or feed.

When they turned onto Main Street, the road was smoother and there were more businesses. They reached a small collection of buildings with nearly identical boxy shapes and brick facades. Kate noticed that many of the shops had no signs identifying what they were, though they didn't look shuttered or closed. The few signs she did see were clearly handmade, all with the same careful printing in blood-red paint.

"The modern frontier," Peter said when Kate commented on the signs. "These people are more interested in the utility of a thing than its decorative value." As he spoke, they passed a flower shop. The hand-painted sign was done in flowing script and surrounded by brightly painted flowers. He grinned and pointed at it. "I stand corrected."

The drive through town didn't take long. "Aren't we going to stop and see if anyone knows about the dig?" Kate asked as the distance between businesses began to grow again.

"I want to drive around a little and get a feel for the place," Peter said. "But we'll stop soon." He turned around and headed back into the center of the town, then turned down a side street. Though the town didn't cover much ground, it had an interesting collection of businesses, including a beauty shop that boasted its own "storyteller" and a tiny gift shop painted bright purple, orange, and pink.

Down each side street, they could only travel a block or two before leaving the businesses behind. The homes there were set closer together, and Kate saw a whole row of tidy brick duplexes. Nearly every home had a pickup truck in the driveway, and several times they had to wait as farm vehicles rumbled up the roads.

Down one street, they barely went a block before they reached a rundown home with a fenced-in yard. A small goat nibbled at the sparse grass next to the fence. Kate strained her neck to watch the goat as they passed. "Did you see?"

"The goat? Yes, but the important thing is that I believe I've found the best place to ask questions about Vanessa and her friends." He pointed ahead.

Kate leaned forward and saw a long school building. A large sign proclaimed it was the home of the Firebirds. "A high school? I'm not sure we should be asking questions at a school. Besides, the school would be out for the summer, wouldn't it?"

"Not the school. Look across the street."

There was a small, well-worn building with a single window. Above the window, a handmade sign complete with slightly drippy paint on the lettering read Pizza Shack. A small, neater sign propped in the window advertised cold soda. "If there'd been an archaeological dig near your hometown when you were a teenager, how much would you have known about it?"

Kate smiled. "Everything."

"So let's see if anyone at the obvious teen hangout can help us."

When Kate swung the truck door open, the heat rushed at her so fast that she expected to hear a whoosh. "By the way, I don't suppose that cabin you talked about has air conditioning?"

"No, sorry," Peter said. "But it's cooler near the river."

Kate certainly hoped so.

After the bright light of midmorning Texas, the inside of the little restaurant was so dark that Kate felt momentarily blind.

"We're not open yet." The gruff voice came from the darkness within.

"We aren't here for pizza," Peter called. "We wanted to ask a question."

Kate's vision slowly resolved enough to see the shadowy figure coming toward them. "We're not the visitor's information center, and we're not open."

Peter sighed, reached into his pocket, and flashed his

badge at the person. Kate's vision cleared enough to see it was a stout middle-aged woman, though the gruff voice could have belonged to a man. The woman's salt-and-pepper curls were pulled back into a messy bun. Too much sun had wrinkled her skin, and the lines deepened when she glared at them.

"Police?" she grumbled. "You aren't local. I know the local boys."

"I'm from Fort Worth," Peter said.

She put her hands on her wide hips and tilted her chin up. "Well, that would make us way out of your jurisdiction, wouldn't it?"

"Not relevant. I'm not arresting anyone, just asking questions. Do you know anything about the archaeological dig on the Brazos River near here? I know some of the young people from the dig come into Elijahville."

The woman managed a cold smile. "Our clientele," she said, enunciating each syllable in a la-di-dah tone while waving her pudgy left hand toward the window that faced the school, "comes mostly from the high school. Those that don't"—she shrugged—"I can't tell you anything about them. I figure folks like their privacy."

"You haven't heard talk about the dig? None at all?"

"Told ya," she said, "I mind my own business. Now you and your lady friend can come back in an hour and a half, and I'll make you a pizza. Until then, I'd appreciate it if you'd leave and let me get back to my work."

"You do much business on Saturday?" Peter asked. "With the school closed, I'm surprised you bother to open."

"There's always something going on at the school," she said. "Clubs and sports and such. The kids need lunch. I provide it."

"A positive civil servant," Peter said.

"I try. Now, about y'all leaving . . ." She folded her arms across her ample bosom and looked pointedly at the door.

Peter ushered Kate outside. The light gravel was mostly ground into the dirt of the parking lot, but it still crunched underfoot a little. "You were quiet in there," he said.

"I could tell she wouldn't talk to us right away," Kate said as Peter hauled open the door of the truck. "The more you talk to someone like that, the less you learn." She hopped up onto the truck seat.

Peter leaned on the open doorframe. "Now that's thinking like a cop. I like it."

"Speaking of thinking like a cop, couldn't we go to the local police station? Wouldn't they know about an archaeological dig?"

Peter looked out across the mostly empty land around them, as if he thought he might spot the local police. "Probably, but I don't know anyone personally in this area, and getting strange cops involved can lead to territory squabbles."

"Well, this stop didn't work out very well," Kate said.

"We've only asked one crabby woman," Peter said as he closed the door. "I haven't even begun to work." He got into the truck on the driver's side. He pulled out onto the road, and they headed to a nearby convenience store with gas pumps out front. "Everybody needs gas, so these places hear nearly as much gossip as bars."

Kate frowned. "Don't tell me we're trying bars after this."

"Anything for the search. We'll buy some snacks and pump the cashier for information."

They walked into the small convenience store and headed for the snacks. Peter nodded toward the register. The lanky guy behind the high counter looked like he might have come from the school they passed. He had a book open on the counter and was scribbling notes on a pad with his right hand. The mop of brown hair falling into his eyes and the scattering of acne on his chin reminded Kate of some of Vanessa's high school friends back in Maine.

"Why don't you ask him?" Peter said softly. "He might respond better to you."

"I'll try." Kate carried a soft drink and a package of chips to the register and offered the young man a smile.

"That all you need?" he asked.

"Yes," Kate said, "but could you help me with something?"

"You having car trouble?"

"No, nothing like that. I'm looking for an archaeological dig that's somewhere near here. It's on the Brazos River."

"Oh yeah. I know that dig." The boy's face lit up. He was clearly eager to help, but a man in a stained white T-shirt stepped out of the back of the store and called to him. "Drew, come back here."

"Just a second!" the boy yelled. "I need to help this lady."

The man strode toward the front counter. "I'll help her. I want those boxes stacked."

"Right now?" The boy looked truly surprised. Then he shrugged and flashed an apologetic smile at Kate before heading into the back.

"You need something?" the man asked.

"I'm looking for the archaeological dig near here," she said.

He nodded. "I heard about them. College kids poking around by the river. They're gone."

"Gone?" Kate echoed. "They were supposed to work there all summer."

The man grunted. "I don't know what they were *supposed* to do, but I do know they up and left yesterday. You want this stuff?" He poked at the bag of chips on the counter with a slightly dirty left index finger, as if he hoped to chase a mouse out from under it.

"How do you know they left?" Kate asked.

"Customer." The man rang up the purchases and announced the price in a tone that suggested he was done with the conversation.

Kate wasn't going to be put off that easily. She pulled her wallet from her purse, then flipped it open to show a photo of Vanessa. "Have you seen this girl?"

He glanced at the photo. "I don't know. A lot of kids come in here." Then he announced the cost of her chips and soda again with an aggressive tone that startled Kate.

She paid for her snacks and then turned to look around for Peter. To her surprise, she didn't see him anywhere in the store. Why would he leave her? She glanced toward the restroom signs on the far wall. Maybe he was in there?

She walked outside. Dipping into the Texas sun made her feel as if she had to catch her breath. She looked at the heat shimmer coming off the truck. Though they'd only been in the store for a few minutes, she was sure the interior of the cab was already an oven. She paced back and forth on the sticky blacktop next to the truck as she waited.

Finally, Peter walked out from around the side of the store.

"What were you doing over there?" she asked.

"I followed our helpful young friend into the storeroom to ask about the dig," Peter said. "His name is Drew Raymond. After our chat, he let me out the back door so his boss wouldn't get mad at him. He told me that he met two girls from the dig, Maddie and Vanessa."

Kate gasped. "Does he know where they are?"

"Even better, he said he'd take us out to the dig site. We need to meet him after work."

"His boss said the team pulled up stakes and left yesterday."

Peter looked surprised. "If they did, Drew hadn't heard the news."

"The boss wasn't exactly friendly," Kate said.

"I wouldn't read too much into that. He could have been trying to hurry you along because they had things to do."

Kate felt a rush of hope. She hoped Peter was right. If the boy thought the group was still at the dig site, maybe she'd find Vanessa there. Now all she had to do was wait. "Please tell me he's not working until midnight."

"He gets off in a couple hours. We'll come back and get him. Until then, how about I show you the cabin?"

Kate felt a nervous knot in her stomach. She closed her eyes and hoped that she found Vanessa quickly.

Four

As Peter had said, the temperatures dropped and the number of trees multiplied as they grew close to the river. After the variety of buildings they'd seen in Elijahville, Kate was unsure of what to expect from the cabin. Her first look greeted her as they drove over the last kidney-rattling bump in the dirt road and followed a turn around a stand of pines. The cabin stood in a small clearing with more pines looming over it. Clad in rough brown siding, its main feature was a triangular river-rock chimney nearly completely covered in dark moss. The base of the chimney stretched the full length of one cabin wall.

"There's no electricity other than the generator. I brought gas for it, so I can fire it up this evening. We could run it all night if we want to."

"No electricity?" Kate said, feeling a surge of panic. "How about plumbing?"

"There's water to the sink and the shower, though you'll have to wait for the generator to heat up the water in the tank," Peter said. "But the bathroom has a compost toilet."

Kate wrinkled her nose. "Like an outhouse."

"Not really. Honestly, you should come in and not let your imagination run away with you."

"Can we even get cellphone coverage out here?" Kate asked. "What if something awful happens? How do we call for help?"

Peter pulled his phone out of his pocket. "I've got coverage, sort of. One bar. No, two. Now it's back to one. But don't worry. If something awful happens, I'll take care of you."

"Unless the awful thing happens to you."

"You know, you're usually a lot more optimistic," Peter said as he herded her into the cabin. She didn't answer because her attention immediately snapped to the interior of the surprisingly neat cabin.

Though sparsely furnished, the cabin was charming if small, composed mostly of one large room. The kitchen area had butcher block counters and tiny appliances. The main part of the room held a small table, chairs, and a floor-to-ceiling bookcase crammed with books. At one end of the room, a futon and two oddly shaped chairs faced the large fireplace.

Peter hauled Kate's bag across the room. "I'll sleep down here. The futon makes a double bed, and each of these chairs folds out to a single bed."

"Convenient if we decided to have a big slumber party."

"Fun as that sounds, we'll probably skip that for this trip. You can have the bed in the loft," Peter said, pointing to the steep, narrow steps that were really little better than a ladder. "I can carry your bag up there since we don't have a block and tackle to lift it."

She made a face at him. "You're so very funny."

"I think so."

She followed him up the loft steps and found the low-ceilinged room quite charming. Most of the space was taken up by a beautiful handmade wooden bed that was topped with a gorgeous log cabin quilt. Despite being the highest point inside, the loft was only warm, not roasting as Kate had expected.

"This is nice," she said.

"And you're surprised? I wouldn't bring you anywhere awful."

"It wouldn't have mattered if you had," she said. "I'd spend the weekend in a cave if it meant we'd find Vanessa safe and sound."

"And we will. Why don't you settle in while I check the kitchen to see what we need? Then we'll head back and pick up Drew."

"Thanks." Kate waited until Peter clumped down the steep steps and then sat on the edge of the bed. She took deep breaths, closed her eyes, and said a prayer for Vanessa. More than anything, she wanted to find her daughter and then thoroughly embarrass her with a huge public hug.

She felt better when she finished praying. She opened her duffel, took out a washcloth and hand towel, then climbed down to the bathroom. The idea of a composting toilet made her expect the bathroom to be horrible, but it was neatly functional with lots of brushed-metal fixtures. Kate pulled her straight brown hair into a ponytail and then soaked the washcloth in cold water and wiped her face.

A rap came at the door, causing her to jump. "I'm ready whenever you are," Peter called through the door.

"I'm ready." Kate smoothed a hand down her sleeveless cotton sweater. She probably should have changed into something a little more conducive to poking around in the woods, but she didn't exactly own a lot of things that fell into that category. At least if she wrecked the sweater, she knew she could make another. Still, the soft yellow yarn made it one of her favorites. She didn't want to ruin it.

"Kate?" Peter said through the door. "I'm going to wait outside."

No time to change. She decided to leave her hair up to help her stay cooler. Normally she liked her hair framing her face. It made her feel less self-conscious. But in the Texas summer heat, it could also make her face melt.

The drive back to town stirred up some of the worry in Kate's stomach again, and she tried to distract herself with conversation. "The cabin is actually really nice."

"You know, I might be mildly offended that you expected it to be a shed. What kind of boyfriend do you think I am?"

Boyfriend.

The word jarred Kate's nerves. She wasn't sure why the idea of it threw her into such a panic. They'd been dating for more than two years. Of course he was her boyfriend. But it felt odd to have a boyfriend after being married for so long. Plus, her marriage had been such a disaster.

"Don't rush to calm my insecurities," Peter suggested.

"Sorry," Kate said sheepishly. "You're the best." She looked sideways at him. "I really do appreciate you giving up your weekend to help me settle my worry over Vanessa."

"I'm not giving up anything when I get to spend time with you," Peter said. "And I must admit, I'm becoming a little worried myself. I don't like hearing that the store owner claimed the dig is deserted. If they left for some reason, Vanessa should have called you."

It didn't help the butterflies in Kate's stomach to hear that Peter was concerned. She fell silent and turned to face the passing landscape. The forest thinned slowly, then gave way again to grasslands and scrubbier trees.

They found Drew leaning against the side of a navy blue–and–rust Chevy at the edge of the convenience store parking lot. He waved and walked over to the truck. "I don't know what you said to my boss," he said to Kate as soon as Peter rolled down the window, "but he's been grouchy all day. He even left early. He never leaves early. He likes to be here at the shift change so he can start us off with a lecture."

"Always good to know we made an impression," Peter said. "You ready to show us the dig?"

"Sure, follow me."

As they drove, Kate peered ahead through the windshield as if she could will Vanessa to show up ahead. She realized how silly that was and settled back against the seat. "Why do you suppose my asking about the dig would make the convenience store guy nervous?"

"I don't know, but I don't like it," Peter said. "The pizza lady wasn't very receptive to questions about it either."

Great. Kate's nerves didn't need the extra tweak of panic from that. Still, she preferred that Peter be honest rather than comforting. Though they took different roads, Kate could tell they were heading in the same general direction as the cabin. She sighed when the countryside gave way to woods again. Though the woods in Texas weren't exactly like those she'd grown up with in Maine, they still felt more natural to her. They bumped over dirt roads and finally reached the site. Even Kate could tell this was where the college group had been working. Poles strung with twine still stood in the clearing, and a few small tools were strewn around. They could see where tents had been pitched, though now those were gone.

Peter leaned forward and flipped on the GPS in the truck. While he waited for the unit to find a satellite, he turned to Kate. "I'm going to save the GPS coordinates for the site on the device, but I also want to write them down. Could you grab my notebook from the glove compartment?"

Kate found his pad and pen and handed it to him. Then she located her own notebook that she kept in her purse to jot down design ideas. It had two thick paper clips on the cover, holding inspiration pictures she had found. She pulled the photos out from under the clips and stuffed them into her purse. Then she copied the GPS coordinates onto a blank page in case she needed to find the site by herself.

They piled out of the truck and looked around the clearing.

"I guess they did leave," Drew said. He scuffed the ground with the toe of his shoe.

"You didn't think they had?" Kate asked.

"After you left the store, my boss told me, but I didn't want to believe him." He shook his head. "It didn't seem like they'd leave without saying goodbye. Maddie especially. I mean, we hung out some, and she came by the store a lot." He shrugged, looking disappointed. "I thought we hit it off."

Peter stopped beside an open hole and waved Kate over. "Do you see anything different about this hole?"

Kate looked at it, then at the others closer to the river's edge. "This one is sloppier and bigger. Plus, there aren't any strings or sticks."

"I wonder why," Peter said. He pulled out his cellphone and snapped photos of the different holes, Drew on his heels asking questions about police work. Kate walked around the edge of the clearing and poked around in the brush.

She saw something glint as she pushed a branch aside. "Hey, look at this." She bent and picked up a small video camera.

Peter joined her. "Someone lost a camera."

Drew whistled under his breath. "And a pricey one. I have one, but not that model. I couldn't *afford* that model."

"Do you suppose it belonged to one of the kids on the dig?" Kate asked. "It definitely isn't Vanessa's. If her dad had bought her a nice camera like this, she would have shown it to me."

"Could have belonged to one of the others." Peter tried to play back the recorded footage, but the camera wouldn't power up.

"Maybe it's broken," Kate said. "I'm sure lying out in the weather didn't help it."

"No, though it doesn't look any the worse for wear," Peter said. "It's barely even dirty."

"It hasn't rained around here in a while," Drew said. "So it's probably not waterlogged."

"It might need to be charged." Peter turned to Drew. "You said you have one of these. Would your cord work?"

Drew took the camera and looked it over. "Probably. You want me to charge it up?"

Peter considered the idea without speaking for a moment and then said, "No, but thanks. If something bad did happen here, I have to preserve the chain of evidence. I need to hold on to it."

"I could loan you my cord," Drew said as he handed back the camera. "We can pick it up from my house."

Kate smiled and laid a hand on his arm. "That's really nice of you. Thanks."

Drew's cheeks pinked. "It's no big deal. I'd kind of like to know what happened to Maddie and the others."

"Me too," Kate said softly. Then she turned to Peter. "I'm more worried now than ever. Where is my daughter?"

"Your daughter?" Drew echoed. "Are you Maddie's mom?"

Kate gave him a glance. "Vanessa's."

"Oh. Maddie's roommate? She's nice."

Peter looked over the clearing, his face serious. "This is all very weird." He turned to look directly at Kate. "We need to find out if the team moved on. Do you know anyone Vanessa might have called other than you? Anyone she would have updated on her location?"

"I know one." Kate pulled out her phone, but it only had one flickering bar. "Reception here is as bad as it was at the cabin."

"Well, I'm done taking pictures." Peter turned to Drew. "Can we go get your cord for the camera?"

"Sure."

Kate kept an eye on her phone as they drove back toward town. She picked up more bars almost immediately, but she waited until her phone found a strong signal. She didn't want the call dropping in the middle. With a sigh, Kate scrolled down her contact list and picked out Logan Lariby's number.

He answered immediately. "Mrs. Stevens," he said, his voice warm. "How are you?"

"A little tense, Logan. Please tell me you've heard from Vanessa recently."

"No," Logan's voice took on an edge. "She hasn't called me in a couple of days, which is really unusual. We normally talk every other day or so, even with her out in the boonies. She said finding a signal was harder than finding arrowheads. I was beginning to think she might be mad at me."

"Why would she be mad at you?" Kate asked.

"I don't know," he said. "Should I be worried about Vanessa?"

"When you last talked to her, did she say anything about the dig wrapping up early?"

"No," he said. "They were finding a ton of artifacts, and Vanessa was really excited about it. She said they'd probably be there for the rest of the summer. I was kind of bummed about it. I was hoping we could spend some time together."

"I went to the dig site," Kate said. "Vanessa isn't there. No one's there, and their tents are gone as well."

"Vanessa's missing?" Logan's voice rose. "Look, I've just finished a shoot. If they need me for anything, they can call. I'll be on the next plane and in Texas in a few hours."

"That's not necessary. I'm not sure what you could do here. We still don't know if Vanessa is actually missing."

"It sounds like she's missing, and I want to help find her."

"I don't know what you could do. Honestly, it's way too soon to panic. At least let me check with the college to find out if there's a logical reason for the site to be deserted."

Logan wasn't easy to convince, especially since it had to be obvious that Kate was nearly sick with worry. Finally he thanked her for calling and asked her to keep him in the loop.

"I will," Kate agreed before she hung up. She turned to look at Peter. "Well, I did my good deed for the day and scared that poor young man."

"I didn't know Vanessa had a special guy," Peter said. "I remember you mentioning him when your friends Alice and Jim were in town, and I know he was here for that charity event last year, but I thought he was just a friend."

"I thought he was," Kate said. "But Vanessa's been talking about him a lot lately. She wasn't exactly thrilled when I made it clear to her that I don't want her to rush into anything."

"If they've been friends for a while now, I wouldn't say she's exactly rushing things," Peter said.

"I'm still worried about her."

"I can vouch for your commitment to not rushing into romantic relationships."

"That sounds like a criticism," Kate said.

Peter shook his head. "More like moping. You know I'm crazy about you, Kate. I wish it went both ways."

"I never said it didn't," Kate said.

"Then it does?"

Kate waved her hands. "I'm sorry, Peter, but I can't deal

with anything but Vanessa right now. And I'm not dealing too well with that. Where is my daughter?"

"I wish I knew," Peter said as his mouth settled in a grim line. "I wish I knew."

Five

Peter followed Drew's Chevy to a small house clad in faded siding. The front door had a ripped screen and opened out onto a cracked concrete pad. The yard was completely bare of trees, and one side was fenced. A little dog with wiry curls peered through the chain-link at them but didn't bark. Drew hopped out of his car, opened the fence gate, scratched the little dog between the ears, and headed into the house by a side door, the dog at his heels.

It took only minutes for Drew to return with the cord for the camera. He handed it through the truck window. "I'll let you know if I hear anything around town about Maddie," he said, then added quickly, "or your daughter."

Kate smiled at him. "I appreciate that more than you can imagine."

Color flushed the boy's cheeks again. "You know where to find me when you're done with the cord. I have to work tomorrow, so I'll be there pretty much all day."

They parted ways, and Kate was sorry to leave her one thin connection to Vanessa. As she settled herself into the truck, she locked eyes with Drew, who was watching them leave. She saw him change his expression from worried to reassuring. The unexpected kindness of this gesture eased her anxiety for a moment. He'd make a good boyfriend. She could understand why Maddie liked him.

"So, what do we do next?" Kate asked as Peter pulled out of the short driveway.

He looked down at his watch. "We might still catch someone in the office at the college, assuming the office is open on Saturday at all. I think we need to get a phone number for the leader of the expedition or someone in the archaeology department." Peter slowed his truck to a crawl behind a farm tractor. "See if you can find a number on your phone."

Kate pulled her phone out of her purse. She was glad she'd finally let Vanessa talk her into a smartphone. After resisting for several years, she discovered over and over how glad she was to have it. The Web pages for Regency College were tiny on the phone's screen, and there were so many of them. Frustration built as Kate flipped through page after page, looking for a phone number in a sea of email addresses.

"Do I need to find a place with Wi-Fi?" Peter asked. "We could use my laptop."

"No, I think I found it." Kate punched in the number, then groaned when a recorded voice gave her the office hours of the department. They didn't include Saturday hours. "I can't wait until Monday to get a lead."

"I know you tried Vanessa's roommate's phone, but can you think of anyone else who might have a contact number?"

Kate's eyes widened and she nodded. "Sure, Vanessa's other roommate, Zoe. The three of them are close. She'd probably have the number, and she's taking summer classes."

"Do you have her number?" Peter asked.

Kate sighed. "No. I'm pretty sure it's one of the backup numbers that Vanessa gave me before she left for this trip, but there was a long list and I didn't put all of them into my phone."

"Do you have the list itself?"

"Certainly," Kate said. She opened her purse and went to the pocket with the list, but it wasn't there. She searched another pocket. Then she dug in her purse and started pulling things out in earnest. "I was sure it was in here." Eventually, everything from her bag was in her lap, but there was no list.

"Not there?" Peter asked.

Kate felt panicky. "I must have taken it out."

"Close your eyes and try to picture the paper. If you can imagine it in your hands, maybe you can remember what you did with it."

"The list was written on a long piece of paper from a notepad Vanessa got for Christmas. It had a blue British police box on it." Kate pictured herself pulling it out of the pocket in her purse, but nothing else came to her. "It's got to be at the house somewhere." She quickly dialed Vivi's number.

Her friend picked up on the first ring. "Have you found Vanessa?"

"No," Kate said. "All we found was an empty dig site. The whole group is gone. I need your help, if you don't mind a scavenger hunt at my house."

"I don't mind at all. I'm home, so I can go right over. What am I hunting for?"

"A long slip of paper with a blue British police box at the top and a list of phone numbers in Vanessa's handwriting. I only put one of the numbers into my phone, but I need all of them. Only I don't know where I put it."

"Sounds like fun. I'll pop over and call you as soon as I find it."

"Thanks so much." She ended the call and looked at Peter. "So much for my detective skills."

"Hey, we all have moments like that. All you can do is solve the problem in front of you and move on."

Kate exhaled slowly and gave Peter a wan smile.

"Let's go plug in this camera and see what's on it." He pulled around the still-puttering tractor and into a small parking lot at the end of a row of tiny shops. They hopped out, and Kate was pleased to note that the heat didn't make her head swim. Maybe she was getting used to it. They headed into the middle shop, which had a small sign on the door proclaiming it to be an electronics store.

"They're certainly low-key about advertising around here," Kate said as she blinked, half blinded by the change in light.

The man behind the long glass counter looked up at them, pushing his glasses up on his nose. He was shorter than Kate, but broad shouldered, with muscles that made up for what he lacked in height. "Word of mouth is usually enough around here. I'm the only electronics shop in town, though for anything really pricey, folks usually make the road trip to find a big-box store. If you're looking for directions to one, I can't help. I'm making it a point to forget they exist."

"Actually, you're exactly the kind of shop I'm looking for," Peter said.

The man's face brightened. "Great. I'm Clark. What can I do for you?"

"This digital camera isn't working, but I think it may be a dead battery," Peter said. "Can we borrow an electrical outlet?"

Kate expected to see disappointment on the man's face, but instead he continued to smile. "I don't see why not." He peered over at the camera. "That's some piece of equipment. I don't carry anything that nice in the shop, so if it is broken, I'd probably have to send it out."

"I'm hoping it won't come to that." Peter plugged the charging cord into the camera and then into the wall. They waited for the camera to have enough charge to turn on, then Peter called up the last images. Someone had been shooting stills with the video camera, and they were very clear and crisp. The first few were mostly sweaty faces grinning at the camera and fingers holding up broken bits of pottery and chipped rock.

Finally they reached a photo of a grinning girl whose long, dark hair was pulled back into a ponytail. Streaks of dirt on her forehead suggested she'd recently swiped at sweat with a dirty hand. She held up an arrowhead to the camera. Kate recognized her daughter's bright smile, and her heart seemed to lurch in her chest, but she didn't comment until Vanessa's roommate showed up in a photo. The tall blonde looked as happy and proud as Vanessa. "That's Maddie."

"And I recognized Vanessa, of course," Peter said. "Have you seen anyone else you know?"

Kate shook her head. So far they'd seen two young men who must have been working with Maddie and Vanessa. One looked barely older than Vanessa and the other was probably in his mid-twenties, with big brown eyes and a grin behind a scruffy beard.

"He seems kind of young to be a professor," Peter said.

"That's not the professor," Kate answered. "Vanessa told me that the professor sponsoring the dig is a woman."

Peter shrugged. "Maybe she's camera shy."

The man from the shop had drifted closer while Peter paged through the photos. "Those are the guys from the dig out at the river."

Kate looked up sharply. "Yes, do you know them?"

He shook his head. "They didn't come in here. I did see the guy with the beard at the grocery down the street though." He smiled a little. "The girls are cute."

"Be careful with what you say next, Clark," Peter warned. "This lady is the mom of one of them. Did you know they'd left the dig?"

Clark looked surprised. "No. Someone told me they were going to be there all summer. As you can imagine in a town this size, they were a popular topic of conversation. I'm surprised they left." He nodded toward the screen. "It looks like they were doing pretty well."

"Yeah, we don't really understand it either," Peter said as he turned his attention back to the screen and continued scrolling through the photos. Suddenly the pictures changed. They were no longer happy shots of the members of the dig. The last few photos were in poor light, and they didn't include anyone's face. Instead, they were focused on the ground, on something sticking out of a muddy hole.

"What is that in the hole?" Kate asked, leaning close and squinting.

"I can't tell," Peter said. "The screen's too small."

Clark turned away from the camera and dug around on some low shelves behind the counter. He set a laptop on the glass countertop. "You can plug it into my laptop here. The resolution on this camera is really good. You should be able to see whatever's in the hole."

"Will it have enough charge to work if we unplug it from the wall?" Kate asked.

"That won't matter. The laptop will power it," Clark said. He unplugged the camera cord from the wall and the tiny screen went dark. Then he removed part of the plug to expose a USB port. "See, it's made for this." He plugged it into his laptop.

Kate shifted nervously back and forth as Clark did things on the computer that she didn't understand. She could handle

Internet searches and knew how to use the word-processing programs for her books, but she was glad they had someone with a lot more computer skills on this task.

Finally the photos from the camera appeared on the screen. As Clark flipped through them, Kate resisted the urge to ask him to linger on Vanessa's smiling face. Instead, she fidgeted with the hem of her sweater and focused on the screen.

They soon reached the dark photos of the muddy hole. As Clark had promised, they were much clearer on the laptop. Clear enough to make Kate shift uncomfortably when she realized what the camera had captured. In the muddy hole, a bone protruded up toward the camera. "I don't suppose that someone buried a dog there," Kate said quietly.

"That looks like a human femur to me," Peter said. "And I've seen a few, unfortunately."

"Still, I guess with an archaeological dig, you find bones sometimes," Kate said.

"You do," Peter agreed, "but I've been to a lot of body dumps, and that bone looks entirely too fresh to be from an ancient burial. It can take less than eight years for a body to skeletonize like that, and the dampness here next to the river could speed things up even more."

"It could still be a lot older," the shop guy said. "You'd be amazed at how preserved some bones can be." Both Peter and Kate looked at him in surprise. He shrugged. "I read *National Geographic*. Some of the top photographers in the world are featured there."

When they flipped to the next photo, Kate gasped. It showed a skull, still mostly buried. The jaw and grinning teeth were clear.

"Unless those ancient people had awfully good dental care, these bones are recent," Peter said. "I think these kids dug up something they weren't supposed to find. I'm going to have to call in local police for this."

"Maybe they already know," Kate said hopefully. "Wouldn't Vanessa and her friends have called them when they found a body?"

"You'd think so," Peter said. "Let's go find out."

Kate stared at the photo without answering. If Vanessa and her friends had dug up a dead body, a few questions loomed large. Who killed and buried someone way out in the boonies? And what was that person willing to do to cover it up?

Where is Vanessa? Kate's mind screamed.

Six

The police station was in a fieldstone building across the street from an electrical substation. The building was so small and worn that it looked more like a movie prop than an actual police station. The barred windows were tall and narrow, reminding Kate of an Old West fort, as if the officers inside expected to be under siege at any moment.

Kate stood beside Peter's truck and stared at the building for a moment. "I'm not sure this place is real." Then she forced a smile. "On the upside, a building that small suggests they don't get much crime. That's a good thing, if there aren't really any criminals around."

Peter stuffed his hands into his jeans pockets and rocked on his toes. "I don't know about that. I think I tend to agree with Sherlock Holmes."

Kate raised an eyebrow. "Sherlock Holmes has something to say about Texas law enforcement?"

Peter's eyes twinkled as he glanced at her, but otherwise he didn't acknowledge her teasing tone. "He found the country terrifying."

Kate looked at him expectantly, so he cleared his throat and quoted the Sir Arthur Conan Doyle detective in an incredibly bad English accent. "He said when other people looked at scattered country houses, they were impressed by their beauty. When he looked at them, he only thought of their isolation and how often crimes committed there went unpunished."

"That does sound dire," Kate said. "But aren't there more criminals in a city?"

"Holmes had something to say about that too. And it's because of the number of policemen in a city," Peter said. "He called it the 'whole machinery of justice' and said in a city, there is just a step between the crime and justice. He thought of the countryside as filled with people who know little of the law." He paused before adding, "Of course, Holmes was never in Fort Worth."

"You know that making me afraid of everyone in this town is not helping me feel any better about Vanessa," Kate said, though she smiled to soften the words.

"Oh, right. Sorry about that."

Kate headed across the packed dirt that served as landscaping around the little building. The small structure had once had two doors on the side she was facing, but one had been bricked over, though the lintel was still clear in the fieldstone. She hoped there was another usable door somewhere in the building, or she could add "fire hazard" to the list of disturbing things about it.

She pushed opened the metal door and stepped into the slightly cooler interior. Inside, the space was crammed with desks, all but one empty. Plywood walls at one end of the room sectioned off the chief's office, another unknown room, and a restroom. At the opposite end, a single jail cell made of metal bars stood empty in the corner.

Not far inside the door, a woman with buzz-cut gray hair and a crisp white shirt looked up at them and smiled. "Can I help you?"

Peter stepped around Kate and introduced himself, showing off his badge. "I need to speak with someone about the human remains found at the archaeological dig on the river."

"Human remains? You mean old Native American bones?" She smiled at that. "Did those kids find something out there after all?"

"They found something, all right." Peter held up a photo of the grinning skull from the camera they'd found. He'd had Clark print out all four of the dark photos of the burial site. "This isn't an ancient American Indian with those teeth."

The woman eased out of her chair, backing away from the photo Peter held. "Let me get the chief for you." She continued to back away for several steps before turning to scurry back through the rough doorway into the office.

"I take that to mean they didn't know about the remains," Kate said.

"Certainly looked like *she* didn't," Peter agreed.

A heavyset man in a white button-down shirt and brown slacks strode out of the office, closing the distance across the small room quickly. He introduced himself as Ralph Slater and shook Peter's hand, then rocked back on his heels with his hands on his hips. "So you have some photos that threw Susan into a tizzy?"

"These were taken out at the river dig site." Peter handed over the photos. "We were out there earlier, looking for Mrs. Stevens's daughter," he said with a nod toward Kate. "We found the site empty except for a pricey camera dropped on the ground. These photos were on it."

"I heard about those kids mucking around at the river," the chief said. "But they certainly didn't call or come in to report finding a body. How do you know this isn't some elaborate joke?"

"This isn't the sort of thing my daughter would think funny," Kate said.

Slater offered her a patronizing smile. "But your daughter

wasn't the only one there. Maybe her friends have a different sense of humor. Seems like kids will do anything for attention these days." He turned to look at Peter. "You say you went out there. Did you see any sign of a dead body?"

Peter shook his head. "We saw the hole, but no bones in it. But we didn't dig for them either. I didn't want to disturb any evidence if there's been a crime committed. I think we need a cadaver dog out there to see if it's a body dump site."

"A body dump?" The chief laughed. "You have us confused with Fort Worth. We don't dump bodies around here. This is a nice, friendly town."

"I'm sure it is," Peter agreed. "But I still believe this warrants investigation, especially considering the entire team from the site is missing."

"Missing? That's not what I heard. I heard they packed up and left. I figured the snakes and mosquitoes out on the river got to be more than those city kids could handle. They stuck it out longer than I would have expected, actually."

"They're missing," Kate said. "I got a strange call from my daughter, and now I can't reach her at all."

The chief shrugged. "Cell coverage out here can be a little spotty."

"So can police assistance, apparently," Kate said. She couldn't believe Slater's attitude. He clearly didn't intend to help at all.

"Hey now," the chief said, "there's no reason to get snippy. I can't allot man-hours and expense on something that's probably not going to amount to much."

"My daughter is missing," Kate said. "A search for her better 'amount to much.'"

"Let's stay calm," Peter said, his voice carrying more

drawl than usual. "We're sorry to have bothered you, Chief Slater. I'll call a friend with the Texas Rangers and see if they can help out."

The chief didn't greet that idea with much enthusiasm. "We don't need no Rangers around here. We don't know that any crime has been committed."

"Then an investigation is in order," Peter said.

"Fine," the chief snapped. "I'll send one of my men out there to look around and poke in the dirt a little. But I'm telling you, those kids are playing some kind of prank. The Internet's full of that sort of thing these days."

"Not from serious students on a research dig," Kate said.

"I'd rather your men didn't disturb any evidence that might be there," Peter said. "I'll put in a call to my friend."

Chief Slater crossed his arms over his beefy chest. "Look, why don't we compromise. One of our locals has a German shepherd trained to hunt cadavers." He turned to look at Kate. "Not because we get many murders out here, but because we get fools who wander off and get themselves lost and dead."

"You'll have the dog sniff the dig site?" Peter asked.

"I will."

"Today."

"It's almost suppertime," the chief said. "I don't know that Russell is going to want to haul out to the river and miss his supper."

Peter crossed his arms over his chest. "It's summer. We'll have light for hours yet. Ask him to carry a sandwich, or I'm calling the Rangers."

"Fine," the man grumbled. "I'll handle it. I suppose you'll want to watch?"

Before he could answer, Kate's phone rang. She saw the call

was from Vivi and excused herself to step outside and take it.

"I found the paper," Vivi said as soon as Kate answered the phone. "It was tucked in a children's book that was on a shelf in your design room."

"Oh, Vivi, you're amazing. It was *Heidi*, right?" Kate said, the memory rushing back to her. "I was looking at some of the illustrations for inspiration for the designs for my new book, and I used it as a bookmark." She fumbled in her purse for her notebook and pen. "Can you read me the numbers?"

Vivi read them off. Kate already had Maddie's number, but she was happy to get the phone number for Kate's roommate Zoe and three people whose names she didn't recognize, though she knew one was the professor who'd sponsored the dig. She'd call them all. She thanked Vivi profusely and then apologized, saying she needed to go so she could make the calls.

"No problem," Vivi said. "Call if you need anything."

"I will," Kate said. "We might be needing Sam."

"Sam Tennyson?" Vivi said in surprise.

"The very one. The police chief here isn't being very helpful, and Peter's threatening him with the Texas Rangers."

"Oh, I have a million questions. I'll hold onto them so you can make your calls. But curiosity is killing me."

"I'll catch you up as soon as I can," Kate promised. She assumed all of the names on the list were members of the dig team, so maybe she'd get some answers.

The first calls were to Kevin Hunter and David Becker. Both rolled to voice mail. Kate left a message identifying herself as Vanessa's mother and asking them to return her call as soon as possible. The third number rolled to voice mail as well, and a pleasant voice informed her that she'd reached Dr. Leigh Usher. "Dr. Usher," Kate said, "I'm Kate Stevens, Vanessa's mother. I've seen the abandoned dig site, and I need to know what happened to your team. Please call me as soon as you get this message."

Almost boiling with frustration, Kate called Zoe and explained the situation.

"I haven't heard from Vanessa or Maddie in days," Zoe said. "But Maddie said they were out in the middle of nowhere and cell coverage was terrible, so I didn't worry—until now."

"Zoe, do you know Kevin Hunter or David Becker or Dr. Leigh Usher?"

"Not personally, but I do recognize a couple of the names. Dr. Usher is the professor in charge of the dig, and Kevin is her graduate assistant. I don't think she's with the rest of the team, though, since her husband is in the hospital."

"The hospital?" Kate echoed.

"Oh, yeah," Zoe said. "Mr. Usher was in a car accident. I heard it didn't look good. I'm sure she must be there."

That explains why she isn't picking up the phone, Kate thought. "Do you know what hospital he's in?"

"Oh, sure, it's the one right near the college," Zoe said.

Kate thanked Zoe again and ended the call. She fiddled with the phone in her hand, suddenly worried that the car accident and disappearance of the students could be related. Then she shrugged off that idea as paranoid, even for her.

Peter walked out of the police department and gave her an inquiring look. "Vivi found the paper and gave me the numbers," she said. "I called all of them. Two rolled to voice mail, but Zoe told me they were both on the dig. Dr. Leigh Usher, the professor in charge, is probably back in Fort Worth. Her husband was in an accident and may not survive."

"Interesting timing," Peter said. "What kind of accident?"

"Car. I called but got her voice mail."

"Well, that might or might not be related to what's going on here. I'll make a couple of calls, just in case." Peter glanced at his watch. "We probably can't do anything else here until after the cadaver dog has a chance to check out the site. After that, I'm thinking we'll be calling Sam and getting some help here. Still, we should have time to run back to Fort Worth and question this professor."

Kate nodded, worry making tears well in her eyes. "Maybe she can tell us where the kids went."

"Let's hope," Peter said. "Until then, try not to worry."

He may as well tell me to try not to breathe.

Seven

As they strode down the clean, brightly lit hallway at the hospital, Kate couldn't shake the feeling that she was farther from Vanessa than ever. She needed to be back in Elijahville, shaking that ridiculous police chief until he took her missing daughter seriously. The drive hadn't taken as long as she'd feared since the professor's husband was in a hospital on the northwest outskirts of Fort Worth. Plus, Peter might not have precisely followed the speed limit.

She cast a glance sideways at Peter. His jaw was thrust slightly forward, giving him a stern look. She knew that look, having had it turned on her more than once. He was in full professional police detective mode. Kate trusted that if Dr. Usher had anything worthwhile to say, he'd coax it out of her. She knew how lucky she was to have him with her. One glance at his badge opened doors that poured out information far more quickly than she could have gotten on her own.

Peter must have noticed her gaze. He turned his head and gave her an encouraging smile, taking her hand in his as they walked. "We'll find her."

Kate nodded. She knew he'd do everything in his power to make that statement come true.

They turned a corner and reached a wide hall with a short row of chairs lined up on one wall. They were empty except for a single person, an attractive woman of about Kate's age. She had chin-length red hair that formed loose curls around her face. Her head was bowed and her eyes were closed.

As they approached, Peter said, "Dr. Usher?"

The woman's head snapped up, and she looked at them with bright, hopeful eyes. When she clearly realized they weren't hospital staff, her expression turned mildly confused. "Yes?"

"I'm sorry to bother you. I know this is a difficult time, but I need to ask you some questions about the archaeological dig on the Brazos River." The confused look on her face grew plainer as Peter spoke. He introduced himself and Kate and showed the professor his badge.

"What would the police want to know about my dig?" she asked.

"Do you know what happened there?" Peter asked.

"Something happened?"

"The dig site is empty," Peter said. "We found a camera with photos on it that suggest your group might have found the remains of a body."

The woman's face brightened slightly. "Really? We didn't expect to find the remains of any indigenous people. That's quite something." Then she frowned slightly. "But Kevin should have told me, and he certainly shouldn't leave the site unattended."

Peter shook his head. "These remains may have been considerably more recent. I take it that Kevin Hunter was in charge of the dig?"

She nodded, the confused look back in place. "The whole dig is really his more than mine. It's in support of his graduate thesis on the technology of the ancient plains people and how trade affected things like pottery making and hunting tools."

"When was the last time you spoke with Kevin?"

"A couple of days before my husband's accident," she said.

"I'm not certain exactly when. He said the dig was going well and that they'd made some solid discoveries."

"And did he sound stressed or distracted?" Peter asked.

"No, he sounded optimistic." She smiled slightly. "Kevin's a very upbeat person." Then her expression turned concerned. "He did mention he was having a little trouble with the other grad student on the dig, David Becker, but he didn't specify what it was. I asked him if I needed to look for a replacement for David, but Kevin said he could handle the situation."

"What do you know about David Becker?" Peter asked.

She shrugged. "Not a lot. He was one of my husband's graduate assistants." Her voice faltered on the word "husband," and she looked haunted. "My husband spoke highly of him, so I'm sure he's a fine young man. It sounds like two strong-willed academics butting heads."

"You know of no reason why the site should be deserted?" Peter asked.

"No, I really don't understand how you could have found the site empty. Kevin said they were preparing to expand the dig site since they'd found so many things fairly close to the surface. They should still be at it. That dig had funding and permissions to continue through the summer."

"Did he report any incidents with the locals?" Peter asked.

She shook her head. "Kevin's a likable person. I can't imagine him getting into fights with anyone. He did tell me that there was something of a parade of locals wanting to take a peek at the dig. Mostly teenagers, but not entirely. I think Indiana Jones made our fieldwork seem considerably more exciting than it really is. Kevin didn't report anyone giving him any trouble though, other than his mild annoyance with David." Suddenly her attention sharpened as she looked past them. "That's my husband's doctor. Please, excuse me while I speak to him."

As she stood, Kate put a hand on her arm. "Could you let us know if you hear from anyone on the dig? My daughter's missing with the others."

Dr. Usher's attention jumped back to Kate. "Oh, you're Vanessa Stevens's mother? I see the resemblance. She's a lovely girl. I'll call if I hear anything, if you'll give me your number."

Peter handed her one of his cards. "My cellphone number is on the back."

The professor nodded, now clearly fidgeting as the doctor neared them.

"I hope your husband recovers quickly," Kate said.

Dr. Usher smiled in thanks and then stepped around them to greet the doctor. Peter and Kate walked back down the hall, giving the professor privacy. They passed the cafeteria sign on the way out, and Peter insisted they grab sandwiches and coffee. Kate wasn't hungry, but she knew it would be easier to stay up with some caffeine in her system.

On the ride back to Elijahville, they ate their sandwiches as they talked about their meeting with the professor.

"Do you think that other grad student had anything to do with this?" Kate asked. "David Becker?"

"It's hard to say. The fact that Kevin Hunter mentioned it at all makes me wonder, but it's too early for wild guesses."

They rode in silence for another few minutes as Kate fought the urge to pull at that thread. She cast around for something to talk about that didn't ramp up her anxiety even more. If she didn't, she'd end up urging Peter to drive faster, and a quick glance at the speedometer suggested that wasn't a good idea.

"You know," she said quietly, more to distract herself than

anything else, "I think I've spent more time in this truck today than in the whole duration of our relationship."

He grinned over at her. "And I hope you know what an honor that is."

"Have I told you how much I appreciate that you don't have one of those window stickers of a little boy peeing?"

That made him laugh. "Believe it or not, I do have one of those. It was a gag gift from my cousin one Christmas. Are you saying you don't think I should put it on the truck?"

"I'm not going to tell you what to do with your truck. But ... *ick*. Those weren't quite as popular in Maine."

"Texans are a little more brazen," he said. "And we drive more trucks."

"And wear better hats," Kate added.

Peter raised his eyebrows. "You think cowboy hats are better than the ones you saw back in Maine? How is this the first time I've heard this? I'd wear mine more often."

"You only have one?"

"Or so." Peter's tone changed then, all of the light bantering tone gone. "I wish we could find out which locals visited the dig site. If I'd planted a body next to the river, I'd certainly check out a bunch of kids digging around it."

"Well, we know that Drew went out there. Maybe he can tell us who else."

Peter nodded. "And since we ought to return his cord tomorrow, we can ask him about it then." He looked over at her again. "Do you want to go to the cabin or stop to see what the chief might have dug up? You've had a long day."

"I want to know what the chief found."

"Then we better find out where he is. I put his number into my phone. Fish it out of my shirt pocket and call him. Put it on speakerphone, and I'll talk to him."

Kate did as Peter asked, and Slater picked up after a couple of rings. "Detective Matthews here. How did the search go?" Peter asked.

"We're coming up to the dig site," the chief grumbled. "Russell moves slower than a herd of turtles. And since this is probably a wild-goose chase, my men aren't exactly happy."

"If this turns out to be a wild-goose chase, I'll be happy to apologize," Peter said. "In fact, I'll be happy in general, because I'd hate to think something happened to these young people while they were in your jurisdiction."

Slater refused to be intimidated. "If something happened to those kids, it'll be the same thing that happens to any kids—wild ideas and not enough good sense."

The cell signal was starting to cut out, but Kate heard him clearly enough. She opened her mouth to respond to the slight against Vanessa, but Peter shook his head at her. "We'll see what you find. I'm heading that way now."

"I'm overjoyed." The chief ended the call.

"I assume it's all right with you if we head out there," Peter said.

"Absolutely," Kate said. "I couldn't possibly sleep without knowing what he finds."

"Good, because I'm afraid that he might screw up the search, so I'd like to be there." He goosed the gas pedal a little, pushing the truck past the speed limit enough to make Kate check her seat belt.

"We're going to run out of decent road shortly," Peter said. "I want to get as much speed as I can out of these last miles."

"Long as we get there alive," Kate said, trying for a light tone but missing it by a good bit.

They were soon off the main highway. The evening hours meant they didn't run into any farm vehicles chugging along.

While Peter had to reduce his speed for safety, they didn't creep along. Still, the time couldn't pass quickly enough. Kate felt every minute twisting inside her, making her wonder anew what had happened to her daughter.

On the more heavily wooded dirt roads leading to the river, Peter slowed way down, which proved to be wise since they had to brake twice for deer meandering across the road. Each time, the deer froze and stared into the headlights, only dashing off when Peter tapped the horn.

Finally they pulled up at the dig site. Work lights hung from a couple of the trees, and Kate spotted four people with large flashlights. One she recognized as the stocky figure of Chief Slater. Two others wore matching uniforms, so she assumed they were police officers. The last man held the leash of a huge German shepherd, so Kate assumed he must be Russell. The dog paused in his attentive sniffing of the ground near the cars to look at the truck as they pulled up.

Peter and Kate hopped out as soon as he cut the engine. "What have you found?"

"Nothing so far," the chief said. "We're dealing with a small financial dispute."

"It ain't small," the man with the dog snapped as he folded his arms over his chest. "I didn't get paid the last time you used Hans, so I ain't moving an inch until someone writes me a check."

"You are failing to give aid in a police investigation?" Peter asked calmly.

He turned to glare at Peter. "What's it to you?"

Peter held out his badge. "I'm a homicide detective with the Fort Worth Police Department."

"Ain't you a little far from home?" the man asked. "You gonna write the check for this search?"

"I will," Kate said.

All eyes turned to her. She saw surprise on nearly every face, as if most of the men in the clearing had finally noticed her. The man with the dog brightened. "Well, that's right nice. Who are you, little lady?"

"I'm the mother of one of the missing young people," Kate said. "And since their welfare isn't enough to get this moving, I'll pay if that's what it takes."

The chief stuck a thick finger in his ear and scratched. "I can't let you do that. If there is anything going on here, I can't have a civilian paying for the investigation."

"If you're not being paid locally, I can call the Texas Rangers," Peter said. "I'm certain they're authorized to handle things like this—missing persons, body dump sites. Those fall directly under their duties."

Slater groaned. "You sure are eager to muck around in my backyard." He looked over at the dog handler. "Have Hans sniff around. I promise I'll get you a check if I have to write it myself. I'll do anything I have to do to get these people off my back."

"Fine." The man spoke to the dog, and they headed into the scene. The dog wasted no time heading for the irregular hole. He stuck his nose eagerly into the dirt, then sat back and looked pointedly at his master. "That's his alert. There's a body here." Russell peered into the hole. "Or there's been one. Looks like somebody might have hauled it out."

"Could it have been some old bones?" the chief asked. "Considering this is an archaeological dig?"

"You saw the photos," Peter said sharply. "You know those weren't old."

"Hans was pretty eager," the man said. "I don't think it was old bones. But when Hans got his training, they told

me that some cadaver dogs can alert to really old remains."
He shrugged. "He ain't got no way to tell us the difference."

"Well, the dog's response and the photo combined are enough evidence for me," Peter said. "I'm calling in the Rangers. Don't mess up the crime scene before the techs get here."

"Swell, the rodeo's coming to town," Slater grumbled.

Kate felt her insides tremble. There had been a dead body in the hole. Vanessa and her friends had found a dead body, and then they disappeared. She was so deep in her worry that for an instant, the loud sound off in the woods and the sudden splintering of a tree near the dog didn't register as a gunshot. Then Peter grabbed her and pulled her low to the ground beside him.

Kate looked into the blackness beyond the clearing. "Someone shot at us."

"I noticed that," Peter said dryly.

Another shot rang out, and Kate buried her face in his chest, terrified.

Eight

The chief had ducked behind the front end of the closest car. He bellowed, "Stop shooting. This is Chief Slater!"

A bullet pinged off the end of the car in response.

Kate heard Slater muttering about paperwork. Then his arm appeared above the hood of the car. He fired his pistol into the air. "Any more shooting, and we return fire!" he bellowed.

There was no more gunfire. The group stayed safely behind whatever cover they'd dived behind for several minutes. Then, one by one, they risked showing themselves. No shots rang out. The shooter was gone.

"Things around here are considerably more exciting than I expected," Peter said as he helped Kate to her feet.

"Only since you showed up," the chief grumbled.

"Aren't you going to go after the shooter?" Kate asked.

"Not without more backup than I have here."

"Can I count on you to secure this scene until the Rangers get here tomorrow?" Peter asked.

Slater gave a grudging nod of his head.

"Then I'll make the call."

"Not from here, you won't," the chief said. "It's a dead zone."

The unfortunate choice of words sent a shiver through Kate. Peter hustled her toward his truck, and they went in search of a phone signal. They found it down the road as the trees began to thin out. Peter called Sam directly and put the call on speakerphone so Kate could follow along. The two men exchanged brief pleasantries before Peter got to the point.

"I've got a problem in Elijahville. I need Ranger assistance, and I believe the locals will agree."

"I'm working a case not far from there," Sam said, his voice sharpening. "Your problem wouldn't be related to meth, would it?"

Peter's eyes widened in surprise. "Not as far as I know. I've got a group of missing college students and what looks like a body dump."

"You found a body?"

"No, but I believe the college students may have. They were part of an archaeological dig." He went on to explain what they'd discovered so far. "I need a tech team out here, and I can't really operate officially this far from Fort Worth— but *you* can."

"Disappearing kids and a body dump might be related to my case," Sam said. That confused Kate. *Peter just told him that it wasn't related.* "I can probably stretch my investigation a little to get a team out there by morning. Then when we discover it's not related, we'll already be knee-deep in the investigation. How many students missing?"

"Four. Including Kate Stevens's daughter, Vanessa."

Kate heard Sam's sharp gasp. "I'm sorry to hear that. Is Kate there with you?"

"I am," Kate said. "Hi, Sam."

"I'll be there in the morning, Kate. We'll find her. The Texas Rangers always get their man."

"I thought that was the Canadian Mounties," Kate said.

"They stole it from us, ma'am."

Kate managed a smile at that.

"We'll find her," Sam said. "Keep the faith, Kate."

As Peter wrapped things up with Sam, Kate looked down at her hands folded in her lap. They were gray-green in the weak light of the truck's interior. She felt numb and slightly dizzy from exhaustion, as if her emotions didn't know which way to turn. Terror from being shot at. Panic as more time passed without finding Vanessa. Hope from more people joining the hunt. Her eyes stung and she blinked, startled when a tear fell into her palm. She hadn't realized she was crying.

"Let's get you back to the cabin," Peter said gently. "You need some sleep."

She shook her head. "How can I sleep when I don't know where my little girl is?"

"You'll sleep because you know you'll be of more use to her if you can think clearly."

She nodded, but she didn't know if she'd ever sleep again. Peter flipped off the overhead light and put the truck in gear, swinging wide to pull out onto the road.

The next thing Kate knew, he was shaking her awake outside the cabin. "I would have tried carrying you," Peter said, "but I'd have never made it up the steps to the loft."

She was too tired to reply and stumbled along into the cabin with Peter's strong arm around her. She made it up the stairs and fell asleep fully dressed.

Kate woke when the loft was bright with morning sunlight and the smell of bacon tickled her nose. She quickly scrambled to her feet and looked down at her clothes, thinking they looked about as good as she could expect after sleeping in them. She grabbed a change of clothes and hurried down the steps.

"You should have woken me," Kate called on the way to the bathroom.

"I was going to," Peter called back. "As soon as breakfast was ready."

"Well, give me a minute to shower." Then she froze and looked at him. "Is it going to be a cold shower?"

"No, it should be fine. I've had the generator running for a while."

The shower was hot and brief. She slipped into a pair of knee-length gray cargo shorts and a melon-colored sleeveless sweater that she'd made years before. Kate carefully folded her dirty clothes and left them on a small table next to the loft ladder. She'd carry them up after breakfast.

Peter set a pan of fluffy golden eggs on a pot holder on the small table beside a plate of bacon. He poured Kate a mug of coffee. "This looks so wonderful, but I don't know if I can eat," Kate said. Then her stomach growled.

"Sounds like you can," Peter said. "Remember, food is energy, and you're going to need all you can get today. I suspect it's going to be a busy one."

Kate took a bite of the eggs and made appreciative sounds. Peter smiled and tucked into his own breakfast. To her surprise, she had no trouble eating.

When they got to the dig site, they found Sam and his team already there.

"Do you ever sleep?" Peter asked as he shook the tall Ranger's hand.

"Lately I feel like I don't." He smiled at Kate and tipped his hat. "Nice to see you again, though I wasn't exactly expecting to see you at my crime scene." He gave Peter a pointed look.

Peter raised his hands. "She was already been out here with me yesterday—*before* we knew this was a crime scene."

Sam grunted at that.

"Find anything yet?" Peter asked.

"The techs started on the hole from your photographs. They already found a finger bone. It was small and deeper in the mud. Whoever cleaned up the body drop missed it."

"Any idea how long the body was in the hole?" Peter asked.

Sam shook his head. "No, but I'm hoping we'll get more information when the techs have had some quality time with their soil samples and the bone."

Kate looked around the clearing again. "I don't suppose you found anything to tell us where the kids went."

"Sorry, no. But we're not done yet." His cellphone buzzed in his shirt pocket, and he held up a finger as he backed away to answer it.

Kate's gaze remained on the tall Ranger. "I thought this was a dead zone."

Peter shrugged and grinned. "Maybe Rangers get better phones." When Kate didn't react, he gently bumped her shoulder with his own. "You holding up?"

Kate turned her gaze toward him. "I don't know. I'm glad we're getting more help finding Vanessa, but I'm also scared out of my mind that we need more help finding Vanessa."

Peter took her hand and squeezed it. He opened his mouth to speak, but then snapped it shut when Sam strode back over and called Peter's name. "That was the chief. Someone found one of the kids from the dig site."

"Is it Vanessa?"

Sam shook his head. "It's a young man. He's in the local hospital. I'm heading there now. Do you want to come?"

"Of course," Peter said.

"Let's go," Kate said.

Sam looked from her to Peter, who held up his hands. "I'd bring her if I were you, Sam. She's good at getting information from young men. I think it's the big brown eyes."

Sam nodded and invited them to ride with him since he'd be driving back to the dig site afterward. In the backseat of Sam's SUV, Kate forced herself to breathe slowly and focus on something besides the panic that was threatening to consume her.

The hospital was a sprawling single-story building in beige brick. A set of double doors faced the parking lot on each end of the building. The only other feature was the row of small windows and the few small boxwoods planted near the doors. Kate couldn't imagine a building that looked less like the tall, bustling hospitals she was used to.

A young officer waited in the lobby to escort them. "Do you know which member of the dig team this is?" Peter asked.

The officer shook his head. "I really don't know anything about this. The chief told me to take y'all to Dr. Lancer."

Kate could feel the questions pushing at her, but she tamped them down and walked briskly beside Peter. His longer stride matched the young officer's and Sam's. They made it challenging for Kate to keep up, but she wasn't about to ask them to slow down. She wanted to see this young man. She wanted him to tell her where Vanessa was.

They turned more corners than Kate would have expected. Clearly the hospital extended much farther back than it had appeared from the parking lot. It was a little disorienting, as if the hospital were bigger on the inside. Finally they turned one last corner and the officer stopped at a nurses' station, where a thin man in black glasses and a white coat looked down at a clipboard. "Dr. Lancer," the officer said hesitantly, "these are the people the chief told you about."

The doctor smiled wearily. "The Ranger, the big-city detective, and the worried mom. Yes, the chief called ahead. I'm pleased to meet you. I wish it were under better circumstances." He looked at Kate. "Are you Kevin Hunter's mother?"

Kate shook her head. "No, my daughter is Vanessa Stevens. I assume Kevin Hunter is your patient?"

The doctor nodded, his face solemn.

"Is he going to be all right? I need to talk to him. He must know where my daughter is."

"I'm afraid you can't speak with him," the doctor said.

He was clearly going to say more, but Kate spoke up. "I know you have to consider the safety and privacy of your patient, but my daughter is missing. She could be hurt as well. I need to know where she is." She cast a panicky look at Sam. "Make him take us to him."

Sam laid a gentle hand on Kate's arm. She felt Peter's hand on her shoulder. The Ranger turned to the doctor. "What is the young man's condition?"

"He was unconscious when he came in. He'd lost a lot of blood. I wasn't able to save him."

Kate looked at the doctor in horror. "He's dead?" she whispered. The doctor nodded.

"You said he lost a lot of blood." Sam pulled out a small notebook and flipped it open. "What was the nature of his injuries?"

The doctor gave them another weary smile, this one devoid of amusement. "Someone had stuck a knife in his back. He was also in a fight at some point in the last couple days, but it was definitely the knife that killed him."

"But you're sure it's Kevin Hunter?" Sam asked, glancing up from the notes he'd made.

The doctor nodded, his face sad. "I met the young man once when he brought in one of the young women from the dig."

Kate's eyes went wide. "One of the girls was hurt? Do you know which one?"

"No, sorry, I wasn't the doctor who wrapped her ankle. I met Kevin in the hospital cafeteria line. We chatted briefly about the dig. I did see the girl though. She was an athletic blonde."

"Maddie," Kate said as relief washed over her, though a sprained ankle wasn't much of an injury compared to Kevin's death.

"Was the victim stabbed more than once?" Sam asked.

The doctor shook his head. "No, and from the angle of the wound, I'd guess the knife was thrown rather than thrust. Kevin would have lived if I'd gotten to him sooner, preferably before someone pulled the knife out."

Peter shoved his hands into his pants pockets. "Do you know where Kevin was found?"

"Up near the Thompson farm. It's a ways out of town. Apparently the young fella staggered right up to Mick Thompson and fell in the dirt. That's when Mick saw the knife."

Peter cut an apologetic glance toward Sam for butting in on his interrogation, but Sam nodded slightly. Peter smiled back and then turned his attention back to the doctor. "Do you have the knife?"

The doctor shook his head. "No, Mick pulled it out. Which didn't help the boy any. I expect the chief has the knife now. It didn't come in with him."

Sam flipped his notebook closed and tucked it back into his shirt pocket. "I'd like to see the victim's body."

"It's downstairs." The doctor pointed down the hall to a metal door. "We have an elevator, but it requires a key, and the stairs are closer. You'll have no trouble finding the morgue once you get downstairs. There are signs."

Sam thanked him for his help, adding that he might have more questions after seeing the body. The doctor nodded and said he'd be on duty until late afternoon. Then he turned back to the nurses' station.

As they clattered down the stairs, Peter said, "Even though we know the cause of death, we should get an autopsy. The body may have clues to where he's been, and where the rest of the kids still are."

"I agree," Sam said as he pulled out his phone and placed a call. "Chief Slater, I'm calling to verify that your people secured the knife that killed Kevin Hunter." Whatever the chief said in return didn't seem to please Sam much. "Then you better check with your men so we can secure the evidence. Also, I need the name of the local coroner." He fished the notebook out of his pocket and stopped walking. He leaned on the wall so he could write down the name. "Thanks. I'll meet with him before I have the body examined by our forensics team . . . Yes, that is necessary. You find that knife." He turned off the phone and groaned. "Knife's missing."

"How convenient," Peter said. "I'm not feeling as helped out by the locals as usual."

Sam grunted as they started down the stairs again. "Actually, this is more usual than you'd imagine. I've worked with some fantastic small departments all over Texas, but I've also gotten a few Chief Slater types."

"Do you think he's doing it on purpose?" Kate asked. "Maybe trying to cover something up?"

"It's a little early to tell," Sam answered. "It's likely incompetence and a natural territorial instinct." They reached the bottom of the stairs and pushed open another heavy metal door. A battered sign bolted to the cinder block wall pointed the way toward the morgue.

When they pushed open the door to the morgue, they found a cramped room with chipped floor tiles and in desperate need of fresh paint. A heavy metal table in the center of the room held what was obviously a body covered by a sheet. A man in a gray suit stood beside the table, flipping through pages on a clipboard. He looked up, startled, as they walked in.

Kate took in his wide brown eyes behind wire-rimmed glasses and his thinning blond hair, turning gray at the temples. She guessed him to be about her age. His suit was tailored—something of a surprise in the small town—and he wore a pale tie with a small gold tie pin in the shape of a horseshoe. As the man fidgeted with the clipboard, Kate noticed a gold watch on his right wrist.

The man's eyes widened in what looked like alarm as they focused on Sam's uniform.

"Is this Kevin Hunter?" Sam asked, gesturing toward the covered body.

The man nodded.

"And you are?"

The nervous man offered them a weak smile. "I'm Derek Hurley. I'm the coroner. I own the Elijahville Funeral Home."

"The town's coroner is a funeral director?" Kate said, surprised. At least that explained the suit. She'd never met a funeral director who wasn't wearing a crisp, well-made suit. Both Sam and Peter gave her a look, and she smiled at them apologetically.

"It's not unusual," Hurley said. "It was either one of the doctors, who didn't want the job, or the vet, who said he was too busy." He cleared his throat. "I have a medical degree, but I've never practiced. I didn't want the pressure of the job." He cleared his throat again. "And you all are?"

Sam quickly introduced them and then gestured again at the covered body. "I would prefer to have some of my own people handle the autopsy of this young man, Dr. Hurley."

Again the coroner smiled weakly. "I have no problem with that, though cause of death is pretty straightforward."

"I'm more interested in trace evidence that might be on the body," Sam said. "Speaking of which, is the knife that was used to kill the victim down here? Chief Slater doesn't seem to know what happened to it."

The coroner shrugged. "I haven't seen it." He pointed across the room to a small table. "The victim's clothes are over there. I was about to look over the body when you arrived."

"My people will take care of that. We don't want to miss anything. We have some missing persons related to this case, and we're hoping he helps us find them."

"Oh," the coroner said. "I'll still need to stay with the body until your people get here. We don't have much security down here." He shifted back and forth nervously. "Someone made off with a body a couple years ago. Since then, we never leave them alone."

Kate looked at him in horror. "Why would someone steal a body?"

"It was a prank," the coroner said, offering Kate another weak smile. "Not all of our young people have respect for the dead."

"That will be fine, Dr. Hurley," Sam said. "I'll make the call now. Once my men arrive, I'll be certain they know to stay with the body."

"Good, good," the coroner said.

Sam glanced at Kate. "I want to take a quick look at the body for any obvious clues. Maybe you should step out of the room for that."

Kate looked at the shrouded form of the young man and shuddered. "Yes, I think I will." She turned and hurried out into the poorly lit hallway.

After a moment, the nervous man stepped out into the hall. "Since they're in with the young man, I can take a little break. Would you like to sit down? You look a bit pale."

"Thank you, but I don't want to go far."

"My office is right next door." He pointed down the hall.

The room was well lit and large with file cabinets on every wall and a worn desk in the middle. A piece of countertop had been placed on top of several of the shorter file cabinets. On one, a coffeemaker gave off an enticing scent.

"I buy my own coffee for this place," Dr. Hurley said. "I'm not here that often, but when I am, I prefer not to drink swill. Can I offer you a cup?"

Kate wasn't sure she needed the caffeine, but the thought of something warm to drink was appealing. Despite the heat outside, the basement of the hospital seemed icy to her. "Thank you. I'm freezing."

"It's nervous strain," the coroner said. "I often find that people get cold when dealing with death."

Kate smiled over the edge of the coffee cup. "I suppose you have a lot of experience with that."

The coroner nodded. "If you don't mind my asking, why are you here? The other two I understand, but you don't look like a police detective, not even an undercover one."

"I'm not. My daughter was part of the dig at the river. So was Kevin. She's missing along with the rest of the team."

The coroner's voice warmed with concern. "I am sorry to hear that. It must be very hard."

"It is. Do you have children?" Kate asked.

He shook his head. "My wife was very married to her job. She ran the local veterinary clinic until our divorce. I don't even know where she lives now."

"Oh, I'm sorry," Kate said.

He shrugged. "Our marriage was a challenge." He smiled at her and made an obvious effort to change the subject, gesturing toward the office door with his coffee mug. "Those two seem very competent. I'm sure they'll find her."

Kate smiled. "I know they'll do everything they possibly can. And yes, they're very good at their jobs."

The coroner cast a glance toward the hallway. "That's very comforting, I'm sure. They seem like a pair you can bet on."

"I do trust them, though I'm not a gambler."

The man's attention turned back to her and he raised his coffee mug. "Wise choice. Never trust in luck or veterinarians—that's my motto."

Kate took a sip of her coffee as an uncomfortable silence stretched. "So, have you always lived in Elijahville?"

He shook his head. "No, I think I've got rambling blood. I get it from my dad. He was in the military, so we moved a lot. But I've been here about eight years." He smiled. "That might be a record."

"Maybe you're settling down."

He shook his head. "Waiting to get the itch to move on. Probably soon."

Kate and the coroner fell silent as two sets of footsteps echoed through the hall.

Sam stepped into the doorway. "I've seen all I need to. I'm going to head out to the farm where Kevin was found." He looked back at Peter. "You should drop Kate off wherever you're staying and join me."

Kate's eyes widened. "I'm not interested in hanging out at the cabin. I'm going with you."

"I made allowances for you at the dig site this morning because you'd already been there," Sam said firmly. "But I'm not in the habit of letting civilians tag along on investigations."

Kate gave Peter a sharp look. "And I'm not going to be left behind."

Peter sighed and clapped Sam on the back. "You might as well let her come along. Knowing Kate, she'll sweet-talk some cowboy into driving her out there, and you'll have one more civilian messing the place up."

Sam looked from Peter to Kate and back to Peter. "You really think she'd do something like that?"

Peter laughed. "You're dating Vivi, and you can honestly ask me that? If the two of them were here together, they'd probably swipe a pickup truck to follow us. Never underestimate the stubbornness of a worried mother."

"You're probably right about Vivi," Sam said. "I guess I thought Kate was the quiet, sensible one."

"You don't know her the way I do."

"Hey, I'm right here," Kate snapped. "And I'm not going to be left behind."

Sam took his hat off and ran his hand through his hair in a gesture that reminded Kate of Peter. For a moment she wondered if Peter's habit was something she'd brought on. Then the Ranger seemed to deflate slightly. "Fine." He pointed at Kate. "But you have to do exactly what I say."

"Absolutely." Kate gave Peter a grateful look as they strode down the hall toward the stairs. The farm would take her one step closer to finding Vanessa. Nothing would stop her short of that.

Nine

As she watched more baked Texas landscape pass by through the windows of Sam's SUV, Kate felt as if they'd done nothing but spin their wheels since leaving Sage Hills. She still had no idea where Vanessa might be. All she'd gotten was more scared.

"Sam," she asked tentatively, rocking forward against her seat belt, "do you have any theories so far?"

He glanced at her in the rearview mirror. "I'm inclined to hold on to my idea about the meth lab connection. The dig crew uncovers a body belonging to someone who ran afoul of the meth dealers, and they're snatched to cover up the secret. Kevin escapes, but is injured in the attempt and dies in the hospital. The fact that he escaped and was knifed rather than shot makes me optimistic for the rest of the team. I'm thinking if we find the lab, we find the place they're holding the dig crew."

Kate wasn't sure she was cheered by the idea of Vanessa being held by a bunch of drug dealers. She sat back and looked out the window again.

When they reached the Thompson farm, they saw no sign of the police. No crime scene marked where Thompson found Kevin. And no one was trying to backtrack the young archaeologist's blood trail. "I'm having trouble believing in Chief Slater's commitment to finding these kids," Peter said as she climbed out of the SUV.

"I imagine his department is stretched pretty thin," Sam

said. "That's not all that uncommon. They cover a lot of land with only a handful of officers, and not everyone gets the most impressive training. I'll see who's done at the dig site and can come over here."

A broad-shouldered man with cropped white hair stepped out of a slanted, rough woodshed and walked toward them. "Can I help you?"

"Mick Thompson?" Sam asked.

"That's me," he said. "I reckon you want to know about that young fella I found? I already told the officer at the hospital."

"I'm sure you did," Sam said. "But I'd like you to go over it again, please. Anything you might remember could help us."

The farmer pointed off beyond the largest outbuilding. "He came from that way. I didn't see any blood at first, but he was walking funny, stumbling. I figured either he had too much to drink or he was a tourist that got lost out in the woods and wore hisself out looking for help."

"What did you do?" Sam asked.

"I called out to him, but he didn't answer. So I walked that way. When I reached him, he practically fell on me. That's when I saw the knife and the blood."

Sam gave him a piercing look from over his notepad. "Did the victim say anything?"

The farmer nodded. "He said 'Help them,' but he didn't say who or where 'they' were. He passed out after that. He was a pretty big kid, but I managed to get him to my truck. I had to take the knife outta his back. I mean, when I buckled him in, the knife would grind in further, ya know? So I yanked it out. He bled a lot more then. I used a shirt and my belt to try to apply pressure to the wound, and I drove like a bat out of . . . " He stopped and gave Kate a sheepish look. "Sorry, ma'am."

"No problem," Kate said softly. "Did Kevin say anything else?"

The farmer shook his head. "He was muttering some, but I couldn't make out any words. 'Cept I think he said 'Hurry' a couple of times. That's all I heard."

Sam tapped on his notepad as he looked at the farmer for a moment. "You said you pulled the knife out of the victim."

"Yeah. I know now that was stupid. I sure didn't help that boy none."

"What did you do with the knife?" Sam asked.

"I gave it to the police officer at the hospital."

"You sure?"

The farmer looked at him in surprise. "Of course I'm sure. What kind of fool question is that?"

"The knife is missing," Sam said.

The farmer snorted. "That ought to be more surprising than it is. Slater doesn't exactly hire the brightest bulbs. I'm surprised they don't lose each other."

"What kind of knife was it?" Peter asked, drawing the farmer's attention sharply toward him.

"A hunting knife, as I recall. A heavy one."

"Do you own a knife like that?" Peter asked.

The farmer nodded. "I own a couple. Most men around here do. Most men I know can dress a deer as well as they can shoot one. Deer hunting puts meat in a good many freezers in this county. Especially these days."

Sam drew the farmer's attention back to him when he handed the man a business card. "If you think of anything else, please, call me."

The farmer looked down at the card. "I will." He shrugged. "Not that I expect to remember anything new. It happened like I said."

"I'm sure it did," Sam said agreeably. He pointed off

toward the barn. "And you're sure the victim came from that direction."

"Absolutely."

Sam thanked the man, and they headed in the direction the farmer had pointed. He looked over at Peter. "How are your tracking skills?"

"I can follow an obvious blood trail," Peter said. "Or footprints, though the ground around here is pretty dry. We haven't had rain in a while. I don't know how well the ground is going to take tracks."

They paced the ground at the end of the barn carefully, but saw no blood drops. Peter left Sam going over the area again. He walked back over to the farmer with Kate at his heels. "You say that's where you saw the young man? I can't find any blood."

The older man shrugged. "Not surprised. The boy wasn't covered in blood. I didn't even know he was stabbed until he fell over."

"How about you show us exactly where he was when you first noticed him?"

The farmer marched over to where Sam was and pointed at the dirt. "Anything else?" he asked.

Peter shook his head.

"Then if you'll excuse me, I've got animals to feed." The farmer turned on his heel and stalked away.

No one spoke until the older man was well out of hearing range.

"Something about him doesn't sit right," Peter said.

"It's possible the bleeding had mostly stopped," Sam said when they finally gave up. "And the farmer got it going again when he pulled out the knife."

Peter turned to look back toward the farmyard where

Mick Thompson was throwing corn to a ragged group of chickens. "Assuming he told us the truth about where he saw Kevin."

"Why wouldn't he?" Kate asked.

"I can think of a couple of reasons, and none of them good," Peter answered.

"Well, I'll get a dog out here and see if we can pick up Kevin's trail," Sam said as he pulled his cellphone from his pocket again.

"That's likely to take a few hours," Peter said. "Do you think you could spare someone to give Kate and me a lift into town to grab some lunch? We might look into chatting up some locals."

"Sounds like as good a plan as any," Sam agreed.

Kate was reluctant to leave the farm. She wanted to keep searching for Vanessa. "What if we kept walking back in the direction Kevin came from? We might run into something, some clue," she suggested.

Sam nodded, pushing his hat back on his head. "We're going to do exactly that, only with a dog. Who knows how many times Kevin changed direction? Blood loss is disorienting. All you're going to do by wandering blind is wear yourself out and let the Texas sun put you in the hospital."

Kate knew Sam was right, and she let Peter gently guide her toward the SUV. Suddenly, she had an idea. She pulled away from Peter to walk over to Mick Thompson. "Excuse me," she said, offering him her most harmless, wide-eyed smile. "Could you possibly do me a favor?"

The farmer smiled at her. "I'm always happy to do a favor for a lady."

"The Ranger needs to stay here until his men arrive, but I'm starving. I know you've already had to drive into town once today under horrifying conditions, but could you possibly give Peter and me a lift back to our truck?"

The farmer cut his eyes toward Sam, then back to her. "I hate to leave in case the Ranger has more to ask me."

"Of course, I understand." Then, to her surprise, her stomach gave truth to her white lie by growling loudly. Kate flushed with embarrassment and pressed a hand to her stomach. "Excuse me."

The farmer chuckled. "Well, now I feel like I'm turning down a lady in distress. We'll have to take my car. The chief kept my truck since that young fella bled all over the seats."

Kate shuddered at the picture that suddenly bloomed in her mind. "I'm sure the car will be fine."

Again the farmer chuckled. "That's 'cause you ain't seen it."

Kate gestured for Peter to join her, and they followed the farmer to the saddest-looking rust-and-navy convertible Kate had ever seen. The car was long and heavy, with a peeling ragtop that matched the chipped paint.

"She runs better than she looks," the farmer said. "Someday I'd like to restore her completely, but the farming business don't exactly leave a lot of money for hobbies. I'm afraid we'll all have to ride in the front. The backseat upholstery could use some work." He opened the passenger door for Kate. She glanced into the backseat and saw that duct tape was doing an inadequate job of holding the seat covering together. "Is your truck back in town?" he asked.

"No," Peter said. "It's at the archaeological site, closer to the river. You heard about the college kids digging out there?"

The older man nodded. "Most everyone knows about the dig. Hop in. This won't take long."

They piled into the car and bumped along roughly on the unpaved roads. Kate pressed against Peter on the long bench seat to give the driver plenty of room; she noticed Peter's grin when she shifted his way. The farmer looked sideways at her. "Sorry about the bumps. I need new shocks."

"That's all right," Kate said. "Takes me back to my childhood. My mom's car was always in need of something. There's never enough money to go around."

"You've got that right," he said.

"So, have you lived in Elijahville all your life?" Kate asked.

The man nodded. "Mostly. Did a little time in the army but came home after. The farm was my dad's and my granddad's before that."

"Were you the only child?" Kate asked.

The farmer shook his head, his frown deepening. "No. I've got a sister, but she couldn't get away from the farm fast enough. Said she'd done all the grubbing in the dirt she wanted for the rest of her life. Insisted I buy her out so she could follow her dream." He snorted. "Not that she's all that much better off."

"Oh?" Kate let the question in her voice linger. She hated to pry, but Peter had taught her that you never knew which information might be useful.

"Yeah, she opened a *restaurant*." He snorted again. "If you want to call a pizza place in a shack next to the high school a restaurant."

"Oh. I think we met your sister," Kate said.

Something in her tone must have bled through a hint about that meeting because the farmer laughed. "I take it Shirley was her usual cheery self."

"Well, we were interrupting her work," Kate said. "I can see why she didn't like that."

"There's always something Shirley don't like." He looked over at Kate again. "You definitely ain't no cop. What are you doing in Elijahville?"

"I'm looking for my daughter," Kate said quietly. "She was on the dig at the river with Kevin. Now she's missing along with all the others."

"Sorry to hear that," the farmer said, focusing intently out the front window.

"Do you have any children, Mr. Thompson?" Kate asked.

"You don't need to 'mister' me, ma'am," he said. "My daddy was Mr. Thompson. Mick is just fine. I don't have kids. No wife neither. But I'm still right sorry that your daughter is missing. I hope she turns up soon."

"I hope so too, Mick," Kate said. "Do you have any idea of where Kevin might have been before he showed up on your farm?"

The farmer shook his head. "There's nothing out that way except woods and the river." He looked sideways at her. "I reckon he might have come from that dig site, but if so, he certainly made one meandering trip. There's a lot quicker ways to get to help from that site."

"I thought you might need some directions to the dig site," Peter said, leaning forward to speak around Kate. "But you seem to know the way."

"Like I said, most everybody in town knew where those kids were digging. It's a small town full of nosy people."

"Have you been out there?"

"Not since the kids took up digging," Mick said. "But I've fished along the river and hunted as well. I know the area."

"Have you heard anything about a meth lab around here?" Peter asked.

Mick's face registered real surprise. "A meth lab? No, though I reckon it was bound to happen. There's not a lot for kids to do around here except work, and it don't seem like many of them are interested in that. That kind of attitude leads to trouble."

Kate didn't know what to say next. She never enjoyed hearing people speak ill of young people, as if their own youth had been nothing but good manners and industry. She remembered her own teen years too well to buy into that. Instead of responding, she turned to look out the window and wonder about Vanessa.

By the time they reached the last turn before the dig site, Kate was beginning to worry about her health from all the jolts and bumps. She was definitely out of the habit of being battered by a car. Finally they rolled to a stop near Peter's truck. Peter opened the door the second the car stopped moving. He hopped out and held the door for Kate.

She hesitated and touched Mick's arm. "Thank you so much for the ride."

Mick bobbed his head. "You're welcome, ma'am. Y'all be safe now."

"I'll do my best. If you hear anything about the missing students, will you let us know? I'm so worried."

The farmer looked at her, meeting her eyes with his serious gaze. "I'll let you know anything I hear." She got the feeling he had something else to say, but the moment passed and he bid her good day.

She thanked him again, then slipped out of the car. Standing beside Peter, she watched the car rumble away. "I think he might know more than he said," she said quietly.

"I think you're right," Peter said. "But I've had that feeling about pretty much everyone we've spoken to since we got here. I'm thinking Elijahville has secrets."

She turned to Peter, her eyes wide. "Do you think Vanessa is all right?"

"I can't let myself think anything else," Peter said. "And you shouldn't either. Now let's get into town and ask some nosy people some nosy questions."

Ten

When they got to town, Peter made a point of driving by the ramshackle pizza joint, but the restaurant wore a shiny, brand-new "Closed" sign on the door. "Looks like Shirley wants to make sure there's no mistaking that," he said.

There were no cars in the small lot, so they didn't bother to stop. They continued on into town and pulled into a small, full parking lot next to a long, low building. It was identified by a sign that read Restaurant, though Kate suspected it was more of a diner.

The interior of "Restaurant" was dark, mostly full, and uncomfortably warm. Kate doubted it would brighten up much as her eyes adjusted. The walls were faced with dark paneling and the windows were covered with bamboo blinds. Large ceiling fans turned slowly, as if the heat inside the building was too much for them to handle. The scent of fry grease hung in the air along with the din of conversation. A sign inside the door invited them to seat themselves, so Kate and Peter chose a table as close to the center of the room as possible.

Kate looked over the menu, hoping to find something that didn't feature quite so much frying. She settled on a BLT as the waitress sashayed up. She wore so much eye makeup, Kate wondered if she had trouble keeping her eyes open. The waitress had close-cropped blond hair with pink highlights, and her white button-down shirt had the sleeves rolled up to show off extensive tattoos. "What can I get y'all to drink?"

"Water is fine," Kate said. "And I know what I want to eat as well—a BLT."

"Terrific." The girl looked expectantly at Peter.

"I'll have the same, but with sweet tea to drink, please," Peter said. "You seem to be doing a lot of business today."

The girl nodded. "Fried food and gossip, our specialties."

Kate raised her eyebrows. "In that case, do you know anything about the young people out at the dig site?"

The girl narrowed her eyes, and for a moment Kate thought she had annoyed her. But then she realized the girl was squinting. Finally, she pointed at Peter with her pen. "You're that cop from Fort Worth, right? I heard about you. And I heard about that poor guy who got a knife in the back too."

"News travels fast," Peter said.

She shrugged. "This place is the hub of the universe around here." Then she grinned. "You found out who knifed the poor guy yet?"

"Not yet," Peter said. "Do you have any theories?"

"I got plenty of theories, but I don't know nothing about it. I better go turn in this order; my boss is giving me the hairy eyeball again." She rolled her eyes. "The man thinks he's the dictator of the Country of Restaurant."

"Well, he is your boss," Kate said.

The young woman looked at her and laughed. "All the more reason to stand my ground. You gotta be assertive, lady. Don't give men any reason to think they can push you around." She nodded. "It's the new millennium." Then she spun and headed briskly toward the kitchen.

"The people around here are certainly interesting," Kate said. She looked over the room and saw most of the seats were filled with men in work clothes with cowboy hats or ball caps. Her attention was drawn to the front door opening and she gasped.

Peter turned to look. "What is it?"

"Him." Kate pointed toward the door. A handsome young man in jeans and a T-shirt stood inside the door, squinting into the dark diner. "That's Vanessa's friend Logan."

"Terrific," Peter muttered. "That's exactly what this investigation needs. An actor."

Despite the sign near the door inviting patrons to seat themselves, Logan was greeted by the same waitress who'd taken Kate and Peter's order. She actually took Logan by the hand to lead him to a table. He was halfway across the room when his face lit up. "Mrs. Stevens!" He practically ran to their table, pulling free of the waitress's hand without seeming to notice. "Have you heard anything about Vanessa?"

"Nothing so far," Kate said. "Though there have been some developments. Why are you here?"

"Vanessa's my best friend. I couldn't stay in New York with her missing."

"Excuse me?" the waitress said when she reached the table. "Are you joining these folks, or do you want me to take you to a table?"

Logan looked hopefully at Kate.

"You're welcome to join us." She caught the expression on Peter's face and noted it was a bit less welcoming. "You remember Peter, of course."

"Yes." Logan sat down quickly, then turned to the waitress. "Do you have bottled water? I would love some cold water."

"Of course. I'll find something." She spun on her heel and rushed to the kitchen.

"What are the developments?" Logan asked.

Peter frowned and crossed his arms over his chest. "I really don't know that we need to be sharing details of the case."

"Logan is Vanessa's friend," Kate said, giving Peter a frown of her own before turning back to the young actor. "Someone found the young man who was leading the dig, but he couldn't tell us where the others are. He died at the hospital."

Logan visibly paled. "How?"

"He was found by a local farmer with a knife in his back," Kate said.

"Have you checked out the place where he was found? Is there a search? How can I help?"

"The Texas Rangers are involved with the case now," Kate said. "Led by someone I know, Sam Tennyson. Sam said they're going to use dogs to track back from where Kevin was found."

"Kevin?" Logan echoed. "I think I remember Vanessa saying that name." He looked around the diner. "You know, maybe I could ask around and see what people know."

"I think we have all of that in hand," Peter said.

Kate shifted in her seat. She didn't want Peter to be mad at her, but she wasn't willing to leave any idea unconsidered. "It's possible that the young people around here would talk to Logan quicker than they would us. That waitress certainly acted like she'd be willing to tell him anything she knew."

"What waitress?" Logan asked, looking around again. "The hostess? I didn't really get a good look at her. This place is so dark after being outside."

"This diner doesn't have a hostess," Peter drawled. "One look at you and the waitress decided to expand her job description." He looked the young actor over critically. "Kate might have a point, though, about that particular girl. I suspect she'd tell you anything—or make something up if she didn't have real answers."

"It still might be worth hearing what she knows," Kate

said. "After all, she said this diner is the hub of the Elijahville gossip network."

"Fine. He should cozy up to her a little," Peter said. Then he turned back to Logan. "By the way, how'd you know we were at this diner?"

Logan shrugged. "I didn't. I was starving, and this place is hard to miss."

They stopped talking when the waitress returned. She made a point of leaning toward Logan as she poured water from a sweating pitcher into Kate's glass. She set a tall glass of iced tea in front of Peter and then set a tall bottle of spring water in front of Logan. "We didn't have any spring water," she said with a smile. "I ran across to the Grab-n-Dash. They had a couple different kinds, so if this one isn't good, I can go back."

Logan turned a bright smile toward her. "That's really nice of you. This is perfect. Do you mind if I ask your name?"

The waitress giggled and then looked down at the front of her shirt. "Oh, I forgot my name tag. I do that all the time." She giggled again. "I'm Annabeth, but everyone calls me Lucky."

"I'm Logan."

"Oh, I know." The girl's voice turned breathy with excitement. "I've seen all of your movies. Do you think I could get your autograph?"

"Of course." Logan's smile never wavered. "Do you think you could show me around a little? I mean, after your shift is over?"

Her eyes widened until Kate almost worried one might fall out. The girl's voice rose an octave and she squealed, drawing the eye of everyone in the diner. "Oh, sorry," she whispered. "Yes, I'd love that. I have to go before the boss comes out. I'll be right back." She turned and nearly ran to the kitchen.

Peter watched her go. "That happen to you a lot?"

Logan sighed. "More than I'd like. That's why I've always appreciated Vanessa so much. She's never acted like that. With her, I can be myself. I'm never 'that guy from the movies.'"

"I know Vanessa values your friendship," Kate said.

He turned a rueful smile toward her. "But you don't."

Kate shook her head. "It's not that. I think you're a lovely young man. But I worry about Vanessa losing her focus."

"And I'm a distraction."

Peter laughed lightly and nodded toward the kitchen. "That young lady certainly found you distracting."

"Sure, but she also doesn't think I'm real. She's seeing whatever role I played that she liked. With Vanessa, I'm real. She sees me. And that means a lot to me. I'm not going to do anything to stand in the way of Vanessa's dreams. I want her to have all the things she wants for herself."

Before anyone could respond, the waitress hurried back out of the kitchen, carrying the sandwiches for Kate and Peter. Her face was flushed as she set them down and turned to Logan. "I forgot to take your order. I'm so sorry. I normally do a much better job."

"That's fine, Lucky," Logan assured her. "Those sandwiches look good. Can I have one of those?"

The girl's eyes turned to the sandwiches on the table, and Kate half expected her to snatch one of them up and give it to Logan. "I'll get one right away." The girl made another dash for the kitchen.

"I hope the other folks in here don't mind that she's forgotten they exist," Peter said before picking up his sandwich and taking a huge bite.

"Well, since you're here," Kate said, "where do you plan to stay?"

"I don't have a plan. What hotel are you staying in?"

"We're not," Kate said. "We're staying in a cabin near the river."

"Near the dig site?" Logan asked.

Wiping his mouth with a paper napkin, Peter said, "Not too far. It would probably be shorter as the crow flies, but none of the roads through the forest are straight."

"Maybe I could rent a cabin like that," Logan suggested. "That would be even better than staying in town."

Kate took a small bite of her sandwich and found it surprisingly good. Apparently whoever fixed it hadn't been quite as distracted as Lucky. The tomato was thick and ripe, and the bacon was perfectly crisp, as was the lettuce. Her next few bites were decidedly bigger.

The waitress brought Logan's sandwich, and Kate smiled around her bite of sandwich as she noticed Logan's plate included *two* pickles and a decidedly larger pile of chips. Logan gave the girl another one of his flashing white smiles and asked, "Do you know where I'd go to rent a cabin near the river?"

"I don't know of anyone renting. I guess you could ask over at the real estate office. They might know." Then she shrugged. "Well, you could ask tomorrow. There won't be anyone over there on Sunday."

"And in the meanwhile, what hotel do you recommend?" Logan asked.

The waitress giggled. "I'd recommend you drive on back to Fort Worth, 'cause we don't have no hotels. But if you drive on down past the feed store and turn right, you'll see the Rest Easy Motel. It looks like a bunch of big chicken coops all strung together. That's all we got."

"Sounds great," Logan said.

Again she giggled. "Then I must not have described it very well."

Peter bunched up his napkin and dropped it on the table. "We really ought to be heading back to the dig site and see what's up with Sam."

Logan's face brightened. "Can I come along?"

Peter nodded at the untouched sandwich in front of Logan. "You stay and enjoy your sandwich. I don't think Sam would be glad to see me drag another civilian out to a crime scene."

The waitress rested a hand on Logan's shoulder. "I get off work in a couple hours. You said you wanted me to show you around?"

Logan's face clouded as he glared at Peter, but he seemed to shake it off to give the waitress another smile. "I definitely want you to show me around. But first, maybe you could tell me how to get to that real estate office so I know where it is tomorrow?"

"And maybe you could give us our check?" Peter asked.

The girl tossed the check at Peter as she launched into directions to the real estate office. Then she stopped herself and suggested she draw Logan a map. She bent over, drawing on a napkin.

Peter shook his head as he picked up the check and headed over to the cashier. Kate hesitated. "I'll call you if we hear anything new," she said to Logan.

Logan smiled at her, though this smile had fewer kilowatts than the ones he was giving the waitress. It looked warmer. "Thanks. And I'll call you later to tell you where I'm staying."

Kate caught up with Peter at the cashier, and they headed back out into the brutal summer heat. Kate yelped when Peter suddenly shouted and ran toward his truck. It took her a moment to recover from the shock and actually see what had upset him. The pickup sat on four very flat tires.

"Maybe we ran over some sharp rocks out near the river?" Kate offered.

"I don't think so." Peter dug a finger into a hole in the sidewall of one of the tires. "Someone did this with a knife—and on purpose. And so I didn't get confused, they added that." He pointed toward the rear of the truck. Kate saw scratches in the truck's paint. "Get Out!"

"Yes, that really doesn't look like an accident," she said.

Peter stood up and smiled grimly. "Well, we've been shot at and my truck's been vandalized. We're certainly annoying someone. I'd say things are looking up."

Eleven

Kate and Peter had to wait for the police department to send someone out to make a report on the vandalism and threat. Kate was standing in the sun, wishing she'd brought her sunscreen in her purse, when Logan walked out of the diner. He saw them with the officer and hurried over. "What happened?"

"Flat tires and vandalism," she said.

Peter grinned over at him. "We're making friends."

Kate shivered despite the sweat trickling down her back. She hoped the locals didn't get much "friendlier."

"That's terrible," Logan said. "But you'll cook standing out here. Can I give you a lift?"

Peter jumped on that. "Can you take Kate back to the cabin? I still have to get the truck towed. I could be stuck here for hours. Once I'm through, I'll return that charge cord to Drew. I'll also connect with Sam."

"I don't want to miss that," Kate said anxiously.

"I promise you won't miss anything," Peter said. "I'll tell you everything I find out."

A drop of sweat dripped from Kate's nose, and she wiped at it with the back of her hand. She turned to Logan with a grateful smile. "I would appreciate a ride to the cabin."

They piled into the low-slung car that Logan had rented at the airport, and Kate gave him directions. He cranked the air conditioner, quickly turning the car from an oven into a freezer. "I'm not quite that hot," Kate said as she wrapped her arms around herself.

"Sorry," Logan said as he turned down the air conditioning. "I guess it is getting a little cold." He glanced sideways at her. "I don't want to overstep, but I think you should know that Vanessa was miserable about fighting with you."

"Oh? She told you?" Kate said.

"Vanessa isn't good at keeping things to herself when she's upset," Logan said with a laugh. "It's entirely possible she told everyone she came into contact with."

"So now they all know what a terrible mother I am," Kate said, "sticking my nose where it doesn't belong."

"No one thinks that. Vanessa appreciates your perspective, but she wasn't sure you were hearing hers."

"I was worried, and now it all seems silly. All I want is to find her and tell her how sorry I am and how much I love her."

"She knows you love her. That's one thing she knows for sure. And I agree with you—I want to find Vanessa more than anything in the world."

Kate glanced at the young man's profile as he watched the road ahead of them. "Vanessa is a little more than your best friend, isn't she?"

He shook his head. "Not to Vanessa."

"But to you."

He still didn't look at her. "Sometimes you have to appreciate what you have and forget about what you don't."

Something about that sentence sounded so familiar to Kate. She sat back in the soft leather seat and thought about it for a while. Then she laughed. "That's from the movie you were in—the one filmed in Stony Point. I must have seen it a dozen times with Vanessa. You say that line in the movie."

He smiled. "I do, but it fits. Vanessa and I are friends. As long as that's what she wants, that's what I want too. I meant what I said before. You don't have to worry about me being a distraction."

"Right now, I'm only worried about where she is," Kate said. Then she sighed softly. "But I appreciate what you said."

Logan bobbed his head, his eyes still on the road. They drove in silence for a while. Then he seemed to shake off the gloom. He started in on a story about the last shoot he was on, involving forgotten lines and an unexpectedly exploding prop. The rest of the drive to the cabin passed quickly, though they did have to backtrack a little when Kate forgot one of the turns in the woods.

"Everything looks alike," she moaned.

"Woods are like that," Logan said. "I got lost in the woods in Canada during a shoot once. I was convinced I was going to be mauled by a bear before I could find my way back to the location."

"But you did find your way," Kate said supportively.

Logan laughed. "Actually, no. One of the crew found me and brought me back. I'm afraid I'm definitely more of an action hero on the screen than I'll ever be in real life."

"Speaking of real life, be careful when you go back into town," Kate said. "I want to find Vanessa too much to suggest you avoid asking questions about the dig, but be careful. We've been shot at, the truck was vandalized, and one person has died. I don't want you to add to that count."

Logan looked sideways at her, smiling. "Thanks. I'll be careful. And I don't think Lucky is all that dangerous."

"I hope she turns out to be lucky for us. We could really use a lead." Then Kate had a stray thought and chuckled. "When Vanessa was five, she wanted to be called Lucky."

Logan looked surprised. "Really? I think Vanessa is a beautiful name."

"It had nothing to do with her name," Kate said. "She thought if her name was Lucky, I'd let her eat the breakfast cereal with candy in it because it was named after her."

Logan laughed. "That's her, all right. Always out-of-the-box thinking. I'm glad you decided to stick with Vanessa."

"We did, even when she wanted to change it to Crystal and then to Ariel." She chuckled a little. "Vanessa went through a lot of name phases. I think all little girls hate their names once in a while," Kate said. "I know I did. I wished my name was Lily." She shook her head at the memory. "I have no idea why. At any rate, Vanessa likes her name now."

When they reached the cabin, Kate showed Logan around briefly. "This is nice," he said. "And way roomier than I expected. I hope I can find a cabin rental like this. I really don't know how excited I am about the motel. I hope it'll only be for one night."

"Maybe it's nicer than Lucky described."

"Yeah, well, I'd better go if I want to check out the motel before I meet Lucky. I'll call you if I learn anything."

Kate thanked him warmly and walked him out to the car. As he drove off, she suddenly remembered the shot fired at the dig site and hurried back inside. There was no point in tempting fate.

She looked around the cabin, suddenly at a loss for what to do. She didn't like the idea of not being involved in the search for Vanessa. Finally, she climbed the steps to the loft and unpacked her bag, hanging her clothes on the pegs along the walls. Then she settled down on the futon and tried to lose herself in a book since she'd managed to pack everything except her crocheting. She wasn't having much success when her phone rang. Kate looked at the phone in surprise. She actually had three bars.

"I couldn't hold off calling a moment longer," Vivi said. "Is there anything new?"

"I'm not sure what we've learned," Kate said as she kicked off her shoes and pulled her feet up onto the futon. "But plenty has happened." She recounted the shooting at the dig and went on from there. Vivi listened without commenting beyond the occasional gasp.

When Kate finally wound down, Vivi said, "I'm glad Sam is on the case with Peter. Between the two of them, they'll find Vanessa. And it sounds like Logan might be really helpful."

"I wish *I* was doing something productive," Kate said. "I'm not doing well with waiting."

"Do you want me to drive out?" Vivi asked.

"I'd love having you here, but you'd better not. If we add many more 'civilians,' Peter and Sam will blow a gasket."

"You're probably right about that, but let me know if you change your mind. I'll be out of here like a shot."

"Thanks, though I don't know how thrilled your boss would be."

Vivi laughed. "It would be good for them to see how indispensable I am."

"I'm sure the answer to that is 'totally indispensable.' Tell me about work. I'd like to think about something besides how worried I am for a few minutes."

Vivi obliged, launching into a very funny story about a group of UFO enthusiasts who called to ask about rates for a conference. "I told them our facility was out of this world," Vivi said.

Kate laughed. "You didn't."

"No, not really, but I thought it. You wouldn't believe how many saucy comebacks I have to suppress at work." They chatted for a few more minutes, but then Kate began to get edgy about being on the phone. What if Peter or Sam was trying to call? She thanked Vivi again for calling and cheering her up. After she hung up, she checked her voice mail, but there were no missed calls.

Frowning, Kate punched in Peter's number. "Do you have any news?"

"Yeah, never have your truck vandalized in a small Texas town on Sunday," he grumbled. "If I weren't a cop, I think I'd still be in the parking lot of the diner."

"I'm sorry," Kate said. "You must be on the verge of heat stroke."

"Maybe a little soggy," Peter said. "But I'll survive. I called Sam a few minutes ago, but he didn't have time to talk. He said he'd meet us for supper. Apparently there's a place outside of town that's a little more upscale than Restaurant."

"Sounds good," Kate said. "Though the BLTs were wonderful, and it is possible Logan made a good connection to learn some local gossip."

"Yeah, let's not tell Sam about that," Peter said. "He gave me an earful about having you here."

Kate's jaw tightened as a wash of anger swept through her. "*Here* is exactly where I need to be. I arrived well before anyone in law enforcement was interested in hunting for my daughter."

"Hey, I'm on your side, though let me note that I'm law enforcement, and I was interested in hunting for Vanessa as soon as I saw how worried you were."

"Of course," Kate said meekly. "I'm sorry. I'm frustrated."

"Me too," Peter said. "But if they're slashing tires and shooting at us, we must be getting too close for somebody's comfort."

"I hope you're right. Do you have any ideas when you might come back to the cabin?"

Peter huffed. "It's going to be another couple of hours at least, but I'll come as soon as possible."

"Thanks. I'll find something to do around here." When she finished the call, she walked over to one of the cabin windows and looked out. She wondered how far the cabin was from the dig site or from the farm where Kevin had collapsed. They couldn't be very close, surely, since she got a few bars on her phone at the cabin but had gotten nothing at the dig site. Still, she was curious to know how close she really was.

Then she remembered that she had a copy of the coordinates in her notebook. Maybe she could use the GPS on her smartphone. She called up the program and punched the numbers into the phone. It immediately found the dig site, and she was surprised to see it was less than a mile and a half away if she walked in a straight line.

Of course, she didn't really need to walk to the dig site, but she couldn't sit around for another second. After all, what if she happened on Kevin's trail in the woods? She'd certainly recognize blood if she saw it.

Kate opened the cabin door and peeked out nervously as she thought again of the gunshots at the dig site. Then she thought of Vanessa and swung the door open, ducking behind the wall inside the door. No shots rang out. She methodically walked to each window and peered out, watching for movement in the woods. She didn't see anything. Then she decided to walk part of the way to the dig site to stretch her legs. At least she'd feel like she was doing something.

Using her GPS to navigate, Kate started on a slow hike through the woods. Then she stopped. What if her cell coverage cut out? Would she be able to find her way back to the cabin? She dug through her purse and pulled out a pad of sticky notes. She'd use them to mark trees along her way. Finally, feeling as prepared as she could be, she headed away from the cabin.

In Maine, the few times Kate had gone walking in the woods, she'd always found minimal undergrowth, frequent shifts in elevation, and a lot of rocks. Here, the ground was rougher and Kate frequently had to pick away branches that seemed intent on grabbing her sweater.

The walk took her closer to the river, and she could hear the water rushing in the distance. The air was much cooler than it had been in town, though she still felt a trickle of sweat down her back, making her squirm.

Slowly, the rushing sound of the water and the quiet of the woods overrode her nerves, and she began to enjoy the walk. It was better than being in the cabin. A couple of times her signal dropped, but she continued on, leaving a bright yellow trail of sticky notes. Each time, the signal eventually was picked up again. Then she stopped as a bright flash of blue caught her eye. For an instant, fear made her heart jump—until she realized the blue was only a jay that grew annoyed as she approached and burst into flight. "Sorry about that," she whispered after him.

As she stood watching the branch quiver from the bird's hasty exit, she realized she was hearing something other than the river. *Voices.* Again the memory of the gunshot sent her adrenaline rushing through her veins. She looked down at her phone and realized she was closer than she'd thought. The breeze had shifted, blowing from the direction of the dig site. She was probably hearing the sounds of the technicians.

For a moment, she hesitated, wondering if Sam would yell at her if she burst out of the trees and into his investigation.

Then she decided that Sam would have to deal with it. This was her daughter. She picked up her pace and marched through the brush until she could see movement up ahead. She was rehearsing in her mind what she would say to Sam when suddenly, someone stepped out from behind a deadfall and grabbed her arm. Kate spun on the stRanger and kicked him hard in the shin, shrieking all the while.

Twelve

The woods filled with the sounds of voices and under-brush crashing as people from the dig site rushed toward her. Kate had kicked her assailant twice in the shin before she recognized what the man was wearing. It was the same kind of uniform she'd seen often on Sam Tennyson. She'd assaulted a Texas Ranger.

The Ranger limped backward, holding up a hand. "Ma'am, you need to calm down."

"I'm so sorry," Kate said. "You surprised me. I didn't see you, and then you grabbed me. I'm so sorry."

Kate heard the deep, warm drawl she remembered. "Is that right, Jake? Did you grab this nice lady?"

"I didn't want her walking into a crime scene, Sam," the stRanger said.

Kate could feel her face flaming as she turned to Sam. "I really am sorry. Someone shot at us here yesterday, and I guess I'm still a little jumpy."

Sam put his hands on his hips, a smile on his handsome face. "I don't think you have anything to apologize for, Kate. He clearly assaulted you."

"Me?" the other Ranger yelped. "Did you see her kick me? Twice?"

"With those little bitty feet?" Sam said, laughter clear in his voice. "Man up, Jake."

"Little bitty pointy feet," Jake muttered as he ducked around them and limped back toward the clearing. The technicians who had edged into the woods to watch the conflict turned back to their jobs, laughing.

"Does Peter know you're here?" Sam asked.

Kate shook her head. "I got a little stir-crazy at the cabin. I had the GPS coordinates for the site, so I thought I'd see how far it was from the cabin. I didn't really plan to make the whole walk. And I certainly didn't mean to hurt anyone."

"Don't worry about it," Sam said, grinning again. "I don't think you did more than dent Jake's pride a little. He'll get over it."

"Have you found anything?" Kate asked as she nodded toward the clearing.

"A few more small bones," Sam said. "But no bits of cloth or any other sign of clothing. The techs are pretty sure that whoever was dumped out here, they were dumped naked. Otherwise we'd see some kind of fabric."

"Unless whoever took the bones also took all the clothes," Kate said.

Sam shook his head. "If they were that thorough, we wouldn't keep running across bones—small bones, but human."

"But no identification."

"From two finger bones and a toe? No. But they're already on the way to the lab in Fort Worth. We'll likely hear something tomorrow. Actually, we're about done here. We would have finished hours ago, but I had to split the crew to send some over to the farm. We've gotten samples from all over. Taken pictures of all the tracks, including some that probably belonged to the chief and his boys, and combed the area for any other evidence. Every bit we found is on its way to be analyzed."

"Did you learn anything at the farm?"

Sam shook his head. "No, and that's suspicious all by itself. We found no blood trail, and the dogs were useless. It's like Kevin popped out of nowhere there. It's enough to make me think Peter's instincts might have been right. The farmer may not have been completely honest with us."

Kate didn't have an answer for that. All of her normal reactions to people and whom to trust seemed to be turned on their ear with this town. Everyone was beginning to look a little shady.

"Well, since you're here and I'm about done, give Peter a call and tell him I'll drive you into town for supper. He can meet us at the restaurant."

Kate smiled slightly. "That sounds good." She looked down at her clothes and picked bits of thorn from her light sweater. "I hope the place we're eating isn't too nice. I'm a little disheveled."

"You look fine to me."

Kate thanked him, but she had her doubts. They walked together through the last of the brush and into the clearing. Everywhere she saw clear signs of people packing up equipment to leave. Tears stung her eyes as she realized that this was the last place she knew for certain Vanessa had been, and it hadn't helped her find her daughter at all.

She waited while a young woman lugging a metal case updated Sam on the last of the soil samples she'd taken and what they would test for. Most of the words didn't mean much to Kate, but she'd never been exactly fond of her high school chemistry class. As soon as the young woman walked away to put her case in the back of an SUV, Kate spoke to Sam. "Do you know where the farm is from here? Could Kevin have been coming from here and walked to the farm?"

Sam shook his head. "I checked that out after we talked to the farmer. I knew it wasn't likely. But there's really no way to reach the farm easily from here because of a side creek that loops out and then rejoins the river. Kevin would have had to slosh through the water twice."

"You didn't find any sign of blood here?" Kate asked. She and Peter hadn't seen any, but she knew that didn't mean there wasn't any.

"There was a drop on one of the rocks that surrounded the fire pit over where they must have pitched their tents. We swabbed it, but the rock had a sharp edge. I imagine someone cut a finger on it." He picked up a satchel that rested on a rock. "If you're done with your interrogation, we can leave."

"Sorry," Kate said. "I feel so useless."

"I understand." He put a hand on her back to herd her toward the vehicle. "Once we get out of these trees, give Peter a call and tell him to meet us, please."

The ride to town was mostly silent other than Kate's call to Peter. She didn't mind. She and Sam both had things to think about. Though she could have come up with a hundred questions to ask about the investigation, she knew Sam didn't have the answers.

They were passing the first small businesses when Kate said, "I talked to Vivi. She offered to drive out."

Sam looked horrified. "I would really rather we didn't have the two of you investigating on your own. That never seems to work out well."

"You know that Vivi and I have tracked down the truth more than once. Maybe you're worried about losing your job to us."

"You've certainly gotten yourselves into deep trouble more than once," Sam said.

Kate narrowed her eyes at him. "I wonder how long it

would take for us to become Rangers? Or do they give us badges after we've solved enough of your cases?"

Sam chuckled and focused on the road ahead.

Kate folded her arms over her chest and watched the passing scenery. She wondered how Logan's afternoon had passed and whether he'd learned anything useful from the admiring waitress.

When they reached the restaurant, Kate hopped out of the SUV before Sam could come around and open the door. She didn't even know if he would open the door for her, but she certainly didn't want him to think she wasn't capable of it.

Inside, Kate was pleased to see a hostess. She was ready for a slightly nicer meal experience. The young woman behind the stand was neatly dressed, and if she had tattoos, they were covered by the sleeves of her crisp white shirt. Sam explained that a friend would be joining them, and she assured them she'd be sure Peter found his way to their table.

The tables had no tablecloths, but the polished wood of the tabletop was clean and smooth. When she opened the menu, she saw most of the offerings were pasta dishes. She hadn't realized it was an Italian restaurant, mostly because she had been so distracted with worry. *So much for my observation skills*, she thought.

A young waiter stopped at the table and filled their water glasses before asking them what they'd like to drink. Sam asked for a beer and Kate raised her eyebrows at him.

"I'm off duty for the night," he said. "And don't worry. This will be my only one."

Kate shrugged. "I'm not your mother."

"No ma'am, and I don't think I'd confuse you with her," Sam said. "She's a bit more like Vivi, to be honest."

"Wow," Kate said, genuinely surprised. "I didn't think there was anyone like Vivi."

"Mrs. Stevens?" Kate's attention snapped up to see the coroner from the hospital standing near their table. He still wore a neat suit, and Kate found herself wondering if he always wore one. That would be hard in the Texas heat.

The coroner pushed his glasses up on his nose and smiled apologetically. "I don't mean to interrupt. I wanted to say hello."

"That's kind of you, Dr. Hurley," Kate said, smiling slightly.

"Please call me Derek," the tall thin man said. "I never wanted the stress that came with practicing medicine. I find my present work suits me. I like a quiet life." Then his smile tightened. "I suppose that's why I move so much. Always looking for the perfect life."

"You said you'd been here eight years. Maybe Elijahville is where you're finding that life?" Kate asked.

The coroner shrugged. "Maybe. Most of the time."

Kate noticed the man hadn't spoken to Sam at all. She wondered at that for a moment. "I don't suppose you've heard anything else about Kevin?"

He shook his head. "I have not been kept 'in the loop,' as they say." He looked pointedly at Sam, who gave the man a wry smile. "Not that I blame anyone for that. I'm a country funeral director and part-time coroner, and this is clearly a big-city problem."

"Really?" Sam drawled. "Kevin was doing fine in the city. It seems to have been the country that did him in."

The coroner gave the Ranger a long, cool look. "A good point, I suppose." He turned back to Kate. "I have chatted with some people in town. I learned the young man spent a lot of time at the pizza place across from the high school.

That place has horrible food and worse atmosphere, but the teenagers love it. It seems to me that Kevin was a little old for that group."

"Yes, he was," Kate said quietly. She was grateful for the information. They could certainly use a clue.

"And who told you about Kevin's social life?" Sam asked.

The coroner shrugged. "I heard it here and there. Not from anyone who wants to chat with the Texas Rangers."

"You know, you can get in a lot of trouble for withholding information during a murder investigation," Sam said.

"And thus I tell you about Kevin's social activities."

"Anything else?"

"Not really," Hurley said. "I did call the people at Regency College and informed them of Kevin's death. By the way, that archaeology professor's husband is out of danger now. Dr. Usher asked me to let you know, Mrs. Stevens. Now, if you'll excuse me, I believe the waitress has delivered my lasagna. It's very good here. Good evening."

Kate nodded as the man walked away. "I don't think he likes you much."

"I thought you didn't either," Sam said, hiding a smile behind a sip from his water glass.

"Try to keep me from finding my daughter, and we'll have a problem," Kate said. "And I can't promise I'll always agree with you."

"I'd never expect you to." Sam set the glass down and nodded in the direction of the dining room door. Kate twisted around to see Peter striding toward them. She felt the little surge of joy that she often felt on catching sight of Peter.

He caught her eye, and the weary look on his face brightened into a smile. When he reached the table, he bent over to brush a kiss on her temple. "That was the longest I've ever seen anyone stretch out putting four tires on a truck."

"I assume you photographed the damage to the tires and the scratches," Sam said.

"I sure did," Peter said. "This isn't my first rodeo." Peter picked up the water glass from Kate's spot and gulped down the contents. "Sorry. I don't mean to be a jerk. It's been a long afternoon." He looked at the empty glass, then turned to Kate. "Uh, mind if I drink your water?"

"Not at all." As she spoke, the waiter popped by their table with Sam's beer and Kate's iced tea. He refilled the water glasses and took Peter's drink order. When Peter asked for a beer, Kate caught Sam's eye.

"What a lush," Sam said.

Their joke passed by Peter, who was still engaged in conversation with the waiter.

"You're investigating that guy who got stabbed," the waiter said. "We don't have a lot of murders around here." He shrugged. "Actually, we don't have any. Our crime waves tend to begin and end with folks robbing convenience stores."

"I heard there might be a drug problem around here," Sam said as he picked up the freshly filled glass of water.

"I imagine there's a drug problem about everywhere," the waiter said.

"I hear that," Peter said.

"You ever see any of the dig team in here?" Kate asked. She quickly fished her wallet out of her purse and pulled out Vanessa's photo. "Did you ever see this girl?"

The waiter leaned over and looked at the photo closely. "Oh yeah. I wouldn't forget her. She came in here one night with a tall blond girl."

"Did they do anything to make them especially memorable?" Peter asked.

The waiter grinned sheepishly. "Other than being pretty? No, they were nice though. Oh, yeah—and the tall girl limped a little. But they only came in once. I think they mostly ate at the cheaper spots." He asked if they were ready to order, and Kate admitted she'd barely glanced at the menu. So the waiter went off to get Peter's beer.

"You think someone took a hunting knife to your tires?" Sam asked.

Peter shook his head and fished out his cellphone. He showed the Ranger some photos. "This wasn't a slash. It's round, like an ice pick. And look at the gouges for the 'message.' They're too fine for a hunting knife."

"So, some vandal is slinking around with an ice pick?" Kate asked. "You wouldn't exactly expect to run into a lot of ice picks in Texas in the summer."

"I don't know if it was actually an ice pick," Peter said. "But it wasn't a hunting knife."

"The weapons are piling up here," Sam said. "A rifle shot at you in the clearing. We dug the bullets out of the trees—it looks like it was a .30-30. A hunting knife killed Kevin, though it's still missing. And now an ice pick."

"Did you ask the chief about the hunting knife?" Peter asked.

Sam nodded. "And he promised to look into it. I haven't heard anything from them since."

"Helpful."

When the waiter returned, Kate ordered lasagna out of desperation since she still hadn't looked at the menu. The two men ordered the same, and they called a break from murder talk until supper finished. Sam and Peter chatted about fishing instead, leading Kate to realize she'd enjoyed the weapons conversation more.

After dinner, Sam went to wash up while Kate and Peter

waited in the small anteroom that served as a buffer zone for the air conditioning. "Why don't you give Logan a call and see if he learned anything from his afternoon with the starstruck waitress?" Peter said.

"Good idea." Kate didn't mind taking an extra moment before diving back into the Texas heat. She pulled up Logan on the contacts and was surprised when the call rolled to his voice mail. "He's not answering."

Peter smiled. "Maybe the waitress is really friendly."

As he spoke, Sam joined them. "Are we having a meeting?"

"Trying to catch Vanessa's boyfr . . . uh . . . friend from New York," Peter said. "He's supposed to be grilling the locals for information, but he's not picking up his phone."

"Great," Sam said. "This investigation needs another amateur detective."

"People recognize Logan from the movies, so he's not going to be associated with the police," Kate said as she tried Logan's phone again. "He figured people would talk to him more readily."

"Undercover actor," Sam said, crossing his arms over his chest and shaking his head.

After the third try, Kate gave up. She looked at Peter worriedly. "What if he's missing, like the rest of the group?"

"It's too early to panic," Peter answered.

"That's what you told me at the beginning of all of this, but it wasn't too early to panic. My daughter *was* missing. And now so is the boy who was doing *something* to help find her."

"Ouch," Sam said, but he didn't comment further after Peter gave him a look.

Peter spoke to Kate in his supercalm voice that sometimes drove her crazy. "Let's drive over to that motel where Logan said he was going to stay. We can find out if he checked in. Who knows? Maybe he's in bed and he turned off his phone because he's exhausted from a long drive. Maybe he's still getting the grand tour of the town. You know how spotty the cell service is."

Kate narrowed her eyes a little but then nodded. It was a reasonable plan. "I'm not sure how to get there from here."

"The motel? I know the way," Sam said. When they looked at him, he shrugged. "It's the only place to stay that's close. I'm not driving back to Fort Worth every night to sleep."

"Oh, right," Kate said.

The drive to the motel was short, which was good because Kate's nerves weren't making the lasagna sit well in her stomach. As they pulled into the motel parking lot, it only took a moment to spot Logan's fancy rental car among the more worn vehicles in the lot.

Then they spotted Logan. Three guys were beating him up.

Thirteen

The young actor was being held by two of the assailants while the third tried to shake off the waitress, who was hanging on his back with one arm and smacking him in the face with her free hand. Logan stomped down on the instep of one of the guys holding him. The young man howled, let go of Logan, and bounced on his good foot. Logan rounded on the other attacker and punched him in the face.

Peter slammed on the brakes of the truck and honked the horn. Without waiting to see what anyone else might do, Kate jumped out of the truck and ran for the group, yelling at them to let Logan go. The boy with the sore foot limped toward her and called her names until Kate smacked him in the face with her purse. "I'm a mother. Don't talk to me that way," she snapped.

"Go get 'em, tiger," Peter said, laughing as he pulled out his badge.

Sam joined them, and his uniform had a stifling effect on all the combatants. Then, as Sam coaxed Lucky off the back of the biggest young man and Peter talked to the limping guy, the third fighter turned and ran.

Peter glared at the limper. "You stay right here." Then he sprinted after the fleeing attacker.

Sam finally pulled the girl off the biggest assailant and insisted everyone calm down. "What is going on?"

"*He* tried to steal my girl!" the biggest guy shouted as he pointed at Logan, who was dabbing at his split lip with a tissue Kate had handed him. "We don't put up with that 'round here."

"I am not your girl!" the waitress shouted back.

"I'm not trying to steal anyone," Logan said calmly. "I'm trying to find my girl."

The bigger fellow glared at him. "What?"

Lucky turned a sulky look at Logan. "He's telling the truth. All he could talk about was this girl from Regency College. He didn't even want to make out."

"You tried to make out with him?" the big kid roared.

Sam had to step between Lucky and the boy.

Kate looked Logan over worriedly. "Do you need to see a doctor?"

Logan shook his head. "I've had worse bruises after a day on the set. We have stuntmen, but we still get banged up sometimes."

"Did you learn anything about Vanessa?" Kate asked.

For a moment, Logan didn't answer. He looked around at the others and then gave a small nod. "We should talk later," he said quietly.

Sam turned toward Logan. "Do you want to press assault charges against these guys?"

Logan glared at them for a moment. "No. It was a misunderstanding."

"Are you sure?" Sam asked.

"I'm sure."

Sam unenthusiastically told the group to disperse, and the kids ran. A few minutes later, Peter walked up, panting slightly. "That kid is fast. I couldn't catch him."

Sam smiled at him. "Well, could be you're getting old."

"Not old enough to know better," Peter said. He turned to Logan. "You all right?"

Logan nodded. "It's too bad you didn't catch that guy."

"Why's that?"

"I think he knew something about the dig site. The one guy was backup for the big doofus who thought I was after his girlfriend. But the one who ran, I don't think he was even friends with the other two."

"Why do you think he knew something?" Sam asked.

"I asked a lot of questions about the archaeologists and the dig today," Logan said. "I got two kinds of responses, clueless and hostile. But when those guys jumped me, two of them only talked about the girl, and one talked about how I needed to mind my own business."

"And that's the one who ran away," Sam said.

"You got it."

Kate looked at the young man worriedly. "I'm not sure you should stay here at the motel all by yourself."

"Well, I'm staying here too," Sam drawled.

"And you have a gun," Kate said. "Is your room next to his?"

Sam shook his head. "I reckon I could get it moved."

"You don't have to do that," Logan said.

Sam held up a hand. "You might as well learn now. Never stand in the way of a mother hen. I'll go get the room changed." He turned and strode toward the office.

"So, what's on for tomorrow?" Logan asked.

Peter shook his head. "I'm going to work with Sam. You two are going to try to stay out of trouble. I think Sam's reached the limits of his appreciation for civilian 'help,' so you need to let the professionals take care of it."

"What exactly are we to do all day?" Kate asked.

Peter looked at Logan. "Do you have contacts among Vanessa's friends? People who might have heard from her during the dig?"

"A few," Logan said. "I met a bunch of her friends when I came down to visit the college."

"You came down to visit?" Kate said, surprised. "Vanessa never told me."

"It was after that '70s charity show that I emceed for you and Paige Bryant," Logan said. "I guess she thought you wouldn't approve."

Kate had to admit that was true. Still, it did make her wonder what else she didn't know about her daughter's life.

"And she may have told her friends things that she knew would worry you and Logan both," Peter said to Kate. He turned to Logan. "So, make those calls and write down everything. You never know what could be important."

"I will, though that's barely going to take the morning," Logan said. "What do I do after that?"

Peter shrugged. "You could go home."

"Not going to happen."

"And how about me?" Kate said. "What do I do to help find my daughter?"

"You give the professionals space to work," Peter said. "I don't suppose I could talk you into going home and letting us handle this? I don't like how many times this investigation has turned rough already, and we don't really know anything yet. If we start closing in, I don't know what could happen."

"Then I'll have to be careful," Kate said. "But I'll be doing it here, not in Sage Hills."

"Look, let me see what I can get done with Sam in the morning. Then I promise to check in with you, and we can consider our next move. Promise not to do anything to get yourself killed before lunch, all right?"

"Fine," Kate said. Peter glanced at Logan, who nodded.

After Peter left to join Sam the next morning, the wait was every bit as painful as Kate had expected. She paced the small cabin anxiously for a while, then sat down and tried to concentrate on sketching some possible designs for another crochet book. Inspiration seemed to be as hard to find as peace, and she soon resorted to pacing again. She nearly jumped out of her skin when Logan finally called near lunchtime.

"I was wondering if you're going as stir-crazy as I am," Logan said.

"I'm about ready to climb the walls. Have you learned anything from the phone calls?"

"I don't know," Logan said. "Probably not. How about I drive out to the cabin? We can go over the notes I made. Then I'll drive us both into town for some lunch. At least we'll be moving around."

"That sounds like a great idea," Kate said. "I tried to talk Peter into leaving me his truck and having Sam pick him up, but I think he liked stranding me out here. He thinks he's keeping me out of trouble."

Logan laughed. "From what Vanessa's told me, he doesn't know how often you and trouble seem to find each other. I'll be right over."

Kate put on some coffee, though she wasn't sure her nerves really needed caffeine. Then she paced a little longer before realizing she was doing it. She stepped outside and walked around the clearing next to the cabin, telling herself that was not the same as pacing. She was relieved when Logan's car pulled up.

As he climbed out of his car, Kate noticed that the swelling of his split lip had gone down, but he now sported a black eye. "Oh my, I didn't realize you'd been hit in the eye."

"The eye and several other places," Logan said. He walked around the car, peeking under it several times. "I should have rented something a lot more sensible," he said. "This thing bottomed out a good four times driving on the pretend roads out here, and I think I heard something scraping."

"Why did you pick this?" Kate asked as she joined him in peering under the car. *Not that I'd recognize anything if it were broken*, she thought.

Logan stood up, looking sheepish. "Habit, I suppose. It's the kind of car I normally rent since I can afford to splurge a little now." He sighed. "If my mom were here, she'd give me a lecture on thinking things through."

"Well, I'm a mom, but I'll let you go without—this time," Kate said. "Come on in. I made coffee."

"Fantastic," Logan said. "I grabbed a cup at a convenience store, but it was swill, and the guy behind the counter was a grouch."

Kate laughed at that. "I think I might have met him."

They were soon seated at the little table. Logan flipped through pages of notes scrawled in nearly illegible handwriting. Kate glanced at them, but the only thing she could read was the name and phone number of the motel that was printed across the top of every sheet. "I'm afraid you're going to have to read those to me," she said.

"Sorry. My handwriting has always been challenging." He read through the notes. Most weren't very helpful. Vanessa was excited about the work and enjoyed it, though she had complained about the heat to several of her friends. "OK, here's something I thought was important. One of Vanessa's friends said she complained about another member of the crew, some guy named David. Anyway, David came up with a lot of excuses to go into town, and he always came back reeking of marijuana. Kevin was getting angry about it last week and threatened to cut David loose if he turned up stoned again. Vanessa was worried about how that would affect the dig."

Kate set her coffee mug on the table and leaned forward, excited. "That ties into what the professor who sponsored the dig said when Peter and I talked to her at the hospital. She said that Kevin had been having some kind of problem with David."

"That doesn't seem like the sort of thing that would make the whole dig team disappear," Logan said.

"True, but drugs are what brought Sam to this part of Texas," Kate said. "The Rangers were investigating a meth lab."

"Whoa. There's a big difference between a little weed and meth," Logan said.

"I know I would be upset about Vanessa trying either one."

Logan smiled and shook his head. "You don't have to worry about that. Vanessa is an extremely straight arrow. It's one of the things I like about her. As you can tell from any gossip magazine, drugs are a big part of Hollywood." He looked directly into Kate's eyes. "It's a part I don't indulge in. I promised my mom, and I've kept that promise."

Kate smiled at him, touched that her opinion mattered so much to the young actor. "I'm glad." Then she reached out and tapped the paper he'd been reading from. "I do think this could be an important clue. Any way you look at it, one of the team was involved in something illegal. Maybe that's related to why they disappeared. If he was buying drugs during short trips to town, clearly the dealer is around here."

"You'll find dealers almost everywhere that you find people," Logan said. "When I was hanging out with Lucky, she didn't add drug hot spots to her tour of the town. I didn't know that might be important."

"Do you think she'd know?" Kate asked. "We could go to the diner for lunch if you want to find out."

"No. Let's try something else first. Anything else. I've spent enough time with Lucky and her psychotic boyfriend." He reached up to gently massage his healing lip.

"I might know of a place we could try," Kate said. "There's a pizza place across from the high school. As much as I hate the thought, it does seem like high school kids would be good sources of information about drug dealers."

"Sounds like a possibility." Logan looked at his watch. "It's early. But if the kids are let off campus for lunch, we might catch some of them there."

Kate grabbed her purse. "Then let's go."

The Pizza Shack looked about as good as Kate had remembered. She wondered if it was wise to eat anything cooked inside. She patted her stomach lightly as they crossed the parking lot to the store, hoping it wouldn't suffer overmuch for the cause.

Inside, they blinked as their eyes adjusted to the light. Many of the rough booths and tables were filled with teenagers. The smells of tomato sauce and grease hung heavy in the air. "Do you see a table?" Kate asked.

"Yeah, come on." Logan wove in and out between the occupied tables. Kate finally spotted his destination, a tiny table not far from the front counter where two teens were holding up pitchers to be refilled with soda.

They'd made it most of the way to the table when Kate realized how much quieter the room had grown. She looked around and saw that nearly every person in the place was staring at Logan, some twisting around to see him. Logan continued on to the table as if he hadn't noticed.

"It looks like we have to order from the counter," Logan said. "Anything in particular you want?"

"No pepperoni," she said. "Too greasy." She dropped her voice. "You seem to have everyone's attention."

"It happens. It's only scary when they stampede," he said. "I'll go order. You wait here." He turned and walked to the counter with no trace of nervousness in his posture or movements. He appeared to be totally at ease with the attention. Kate couldn't imagine living that way. She knew she'd be a wreck.

She saw Logan chat with a couple of people who were brave enough to come and talk with him. Each time, he leaned in close to the person as if he or she was the sole focus of his interest. She even saw him sign an autograph for one girl.

When he reached the front of the line at the counter, Kate recognized the scowling woman who took his order. Clearly the Pizza Shack's owner wasn't any friendlier to customers than she'd been to Peter and her. She looked the woman over, trying to see any resemblance to the farmer who found Kevin. For siblings, they were about as different as Kate could imagine.

Logan came back to the table while they waited for their pizza.

Kate spoke quietly to him. "I saw you had a chance to chat. Anyone offer a drug connection?"

Something about her question seemed to amuse Logan. But then his face sobered, and he shook his head. "No, not that they'd tell me about. I hope the pizza is good, because it looks like this might be a bust."

Kate was startled when the owner stomped out from

around the counter with their pizza in her hands. She practically slammed it down on their table. "Eat up and get out. I heard about how much trouble you've been stirring up around here. I don't need none of that."

Kate looked at the woman's angry face. "I assure you—"

"I don't need any assurance," the woman snapped. "I do need the two of you to eat and get out." She turned and stomped back over to the counter, grabbed a pitcher of soda, and slammed it down on their table hard enough to slosh some over the edge. "No tip necessary," she said.

"We wouldn't dream of it," Kate snapped back.

The two women glared at each other for a moment, and for once Kate was determined not to back down. To her amazement, the other woman's eyes dropped first and she turned back to her counter.

"All I want is to find my daughter!" Kate yelled after her.

The whole room fell silent at that. The owner turned and looked directly at Kate. "You won't find her here."

Before Kate could respond, the woman was back behind the counter. She refused to look in their direction again for the rest of the time they were there. The pizza tasted better than Kate expected, but she lost her appetite between the teenagers staring and the owner glaring. Like most young people, Logan showed no such squeamishness and ate an impressive amount.

When he was finally full, Kate was glad to leave. As per instructions, she left no tip.

For once, Kate didn't mind being out in the hot sun. But as they walked to the car, Logan yelped.

"I left my car keys on the table," he said. "The key fob is bulky, so I took it out of my pocket. I'll be right back."

He spun and raced back into the little building before

Kate could even comment. She stood next to the car, looking across the street at the high school.

"Excuse me?"

Kate turned to face a teenage girl with huge blue eyes behind thick-rimmed glasses. She had a denim hobo bag decorated with buttons and pins slung over one shoulder. "You're a friend of Logan Lariby?"

Kate nodded. "He'll be out in a minute, if you want an autograph."

"Oh no," the girl said. "I mean, yes, that would be awesome, but that's not why I came over. I heard him asking about something in there."

"About drugs," Kate said.

The girl's eyes widened behind her glasses. "Uh, yeah. Anyway, you're the mom of one of the guys at the dig site?"

"One of the girls actually," Kate said. "Vanessa. Did you know any of the students from out there?"

The girl shifted slightly and fidgeted with the strap on her bag. "I might know something."

Kate felt a race of excitement. "What?"

"I'll show it to Logan, but only to Logan. I'm sorry, but if he wants to show it to you, that's up to him."

"That would be fine," Kate said. "He'll be out in a minute."

"I can't wait," the girl said. Her twitchiness seemed ready to launch her into the air. She shoved a grubby piece of folded paper at Kate. "Give him this." Then she turned and ran across the road toward the school.

"Wait!" Kate yelled after her, but the girl never slowed down. Kate knew she couldn't follow her onto a high school campus, not with the security that schools had these days. She looked down at the wadded paper in her hands and wondered what secret the girl had to share.

Fourteen

When Logan returned, Kate handed him the folded paper. She'd resisted looking at it, even though she'd really wanted to. She knew he'd show her.

"What's this?"

"A girl handed it to me. She said she might know something," Kate said. "She mentioned drugs and the dig team."

Logan's face lit up. "A lead then." He opened the paper and frowned at it. "She says she wants to meet me after school, and she'll show me something important."

"So we have to hang around here until school's out?" Kate asked.

Logan shook his head. "No, she gave me GPS coordinates and a time, three hours from now." He looked over at the school. "What did she look like?"

"Young, thin, big glasses, and blue eyes," Kate said.

"I don't think I talked to anyone like that inside," he said. "So why is she leaving me notes? Do you think this might be a trap? Maybe we should call Peter or Sam? I'm not really interested in another black eye."

"We could call them," Kate said slowly. "But they wouldn't let us anywhere near that meeting. They'd go out there without us."

"Which means the girl might not show and we wouldn't learn what she knows," Logan said. "Which can mean missing a chance to find Vanessa."

"That's what I thought. Still, going out there without

anyone knowing where we went might not be wise."

"We have time," Logan said. "We can go back to the cabin and leave a note."

Kate agreed, though she wondered if anyone would find the note before she and Logan found more trouble than they could handle. Still, it was worth the risk. She felt the passing of time like a weight in her chest. She knew that statistically, a missing teen was found in the first couple of days or it was too late. This was the fourth day Vanessa had been missing. She couldn't waste time waiting for Peter and Sam to decide to include her.

When they were finally on the way to the coordinates the girl had scrawled on the paper, Kate sat in the passenger seat of Logan's rental car with one hand on the dash and one on the door. The car's suspension managed to smooth out the ride quite a bit, but every time the undercarriage scraped the road, it tightened Kate's nerves a little more.

Logan glanced over at her. "Am I going too fast?"

She shook her head. "It's fine."

"You don't look like it's fine."

"Just nerves," Kate said. "A mixture of this road and visions of how Peter's going to react to that note."

"With luck, this trip will give us a real lead," Logan said. "That should help."

"Knowing Peter, I wouldn't count on it," Kate said.

They bounced along awhile longer before Logan slowed to a stop. "I think I better meet this girl alone."

"Now *you're* putting me out?"

"From the GPS, it looks like the coordinates are right around this bend." He pointed to a spot off the road where a tree had fallen and was covered with low brush. "Why don't you watch from there? If it looks fine, I'll wave you over. If not, you can call in the cavalry."

Kate huffed, annoyed, but she recognized that Logan's plan was smarter than both of them rushing into potential danger. "Fine. But be careful."

Logan offered her his Hollywood grin. "Always."

"Right."

Kate hopped out of the car and shut the door as quietly as she could. She headed for the deadfall as he drove off, wincing each time a twig crackled under her feet. Finally she reached the fallen tree and peered over it. Sure enough, she could see the clearing where Logan's car sat. The young actor stood at the front bumper, talking to the teenager from the Pizza Shack.

"I wasn't sure if you'd come," the girl said, her voice only a few decibels lower than a squeal. Logan responded, but since he spoke more quietly, Kate couldn't understand his words. She wondered if she should try to creep closer in case the girl chose to stop conversing at a screech.

"No!" the girl shrieked. "I do know something. I know where one of the diggers was buying. I can show you the grow house. But you have to drive." She waved her hand toward a ragged motorbike. "My ride doesn't work for two."

"Fine, I'll drive," Logan said, his voice loud and clear.

Kate waited for him to wave her over to join them, but instead, he opened the car door for the girl. She assumed he'd wave at her once the girl was in the car, so Kate started scrambling through the brush. Logan glanced in her direction, shook his head in a small, quick movement, got into the car, and drove off. Kate yelled his name, but he left without her.

She flipped open her phone, begging for this to be one of the spots where she could get a signal. It wasn't. "Fine. Time to improvise." She climbed onto the battered motorbike. She hadn't ridden anything like it since she was a teenager dating Harry. He'd had a motorcycle, though his parents had given him a car when he "settled down" with Kate.

The motorbike was a far cry from Harry's motorcycle, but she knew the basics and got it running. She lengthened the strap on her purse enough to sling it across her chest and leave her hands free. Then she headed down the road after Logan. She had no dream of catching up to him on the puttering bike, but she'd at least be heading in the right direction when she finally got a signal to call Peter.

If she'd thought the road was rough in a car, the motorbike seemed determined to rattle her teeth loose as it bounced and rumbled over the rocks and potholes. At least she wasn't in danger of losing Logan for a while, since she seemed to be on the only road that could accommodate a car. Plus, the dust Logan's car kicked up, even at the slow pace she knew he was going in his rental, made them easy enough to follow.

Finally she reached a division in the road. She stopped to consider which way to go and tried her phone. To her shock, she got a signal. She quickly called Peter.

He greeted her warmly. "I know you must be bored, but I'll make it up to you. I promise."

"I'm not bored," Kate said. "But I am maybe in a little trouble."

Peter's voice cooled and sharpened. "What?"

As quickly as possible, Kate updated him on what Logan

had learned and what they'd done about it. "You should have called me," Peter growled.

"So we could be left out of it?" Kate asked.

"Yes," Peter snapped. "That's where civilians belong—out of the investigation."

"I'm not a civilian," Kate shot back. "I'm Vanessa's mother. Now do you want to come and help me find Logan or not?"

"I'm coming. I can track the GPS on your phone."

"You can?" Kate said, surprised.

Peter's voice took on a breathy quality, as if he were walking rapidly while talking to her. "Of course. I finally figured out that I can't count on you to stay out of trouble. And I can't keep you safe if I can't find you."

"Maybe you should follow Logan's GPS," Kate suggested.

"His is going to be harder; I don't have an app for that. I'll have Sam see what he can do. But I'm on my way. Don't do anything else crazy." Before she could answer, he ended the call.

Kate slipped the phone back into her purse and then climbed off the bike to look down each branch of the road. Both appeared to have seen little traffic, but one had more dust kicked up. Plus, a car had clipped the brush on one side of the road, snapping a small branch on a tree. The break was still bright green. "I don't know if you did that on purpose, Logan Lariby," Kate whispered. "But if so, good boy."

She headed down the road, intent on leading Peter as close to Logan as she possibly could. Though she pushed the bike as hard as she could, she still felt like she was going too slowly.

The little bike's motor was far from quiet, putting out more noise than speed. Because of that, Kate didn't hear the sound of another vehicle until it was practically on top of her. She shrieked as she pulled off the road, dropping the bike accidentally into a narrow ditch.

The pickup truck slammed to a stop, and the driver's door flew open. "Kate!"

She scrambled out from under the bike, moaning at the site of the deep tear and long streaks of grease on the right leg of her pale slacks.

Peter grabbed her arm, practically lifting her into the air. "Are you hurt?"

"No, I'm fine." She pointed. "Logan went that way. I'm sure of it."

"Then that's the way we'll go. Get in the truck."

Kate wasn't sure she liked his tone, but there wasn't time for an argument, so she hurried to do as he directed. They moved considerably faster in the truck than on the motorbike, and Kate again rode with one hand on the dash and one gripping the armrest as she leaned forward, watching the road for any sign of Logan's car.

"How did the girl seem?" Peter said. "Did you get any kind of bad feeling from her?"

Kate shook her head. "She seemed totally smitten with Logan."

"Let's hope that's reason enough not to lead him into something ugly," Peter said.

Kate jumped when Peter's phone rang. He took it from his shirt pocket and put it on speakerphone. "I've got Kate," he said.

Kate heard Sam's warm voice. "Is she OK?"

"She's fine. Did you track down Logan?"

"I did. The car isn't moving anymore. They're near the river."

"In walking distance to Mick Thompson's farm?" Peter asked.

"I thought the same thing," Sam said. "But I can't see any way a man with a knife in his back could walk from there to the farm."

"Let me have the coordinates," Peter said. "I can see how close we are."

Sam passed them along, and Kate punched them into her phone. They were close.

"Look, I don't want to risk Logan, but you need to let me and my guys get there first," Sam said. "This could be more than it appears. I don't want to put Kate in danger, and I don't want to fill out the paperwork if a Fort Worth homicide detective gets killed out there."

The road divided again, though Kate could see that one branch only went a few yards before it dead-ended at a fallen tree. The GPS showed that Logan had gone down the other branch and stopped beyond the next sharp turn. Peter pulled the truck down the short branch and stopped. "I'm off the road. I'll have Kate wait in the truck, but I'm going in on foot. I have to see if Logan is all right."

Sam huffed. "I'm not comfortable with this compromise."

"It's the best I have to offer. Kate waits. I go."

"Fine, we'll be there soon. Really soon. Don't engage without backup."

"I'll do my best," Peter said.

"You're not leaving me in the truck," Kate said. "What if Vanessa's out there?"

"I am leaving you in the truck." To Kate's shock, Peter pulled out his handcuffs and grabbed her wrist. As she tried to pull her arm back, he snapped one loop of the cuff to her wrist and the other to the steering wheel. "I'll be right back."

Kate jerked her wrist, making the cuff rattle. "Don't do this."

Peter leaned over and gave her a quick kiss on the cheek. "See you soon."

He slipped through the brush that separated the two

branches of the road and walked out of sight. Kate flipped open the truck's glove box and rooted around, looking for something she might use to force the lock on the cuffs. She'd seen people on television pick handcuffs with a piece of wire plenty of times. Unfortunately, the glove box didn't contain a piece of wire, and she wasn't wearing any hairpins.

She growled under her breath and took a closer look at the cuffs. Peter had been careful not to pinch the cuff too tight and risk hurting her, but she still couldn't slip her hand out. She pulled out her phone and was grateful for the strong signal. She did a quick Web search on breaking out of handcuffs. To her surprise, she found several tutorials, though most depended on a bobby pin. Then she discovered one that suggested a paper clip was as good as a bobby pin. Kate groaned. "I'm an idiot." She rooted through her purse, pulled out her notebook, and slipped off the paper clip.

Since the tutorial included a helpful video, Kate was able to bend her paper clip into the right shape and fish around in the handcuff lock. The video had made the lock picking look easier than it was, but she finally felt the lock tumble. She couldn't believe it. She'd actually done it. She freed her wrist.

Minutes passed, and she comforted herself by noting that if Peter had needed to shoot his way out of a situation, the sound would have carried. Surely that meant he was all right. Then she remembered that Kevin had died from a knife, and knives didn't make any noise. Kate hopped out of the truck as she pushed away the mental image of Peter with a knife in his chest. She hurried through the brush along the side of the road, whispering a prayer for Vanessa, Peter, and Logan's safety.

At the turn in the road, Kate saw Logan's car. The driver's

door was open, but no one was inside. Beyond the car, an ancient Airstream trailer took up most of the clearing. Now in direct view of the trailer, Kate could hear angry voices coming from within. She had started for the trailer when someone grabbed her from behind and dragged her back into the brush.

Fifteen

"It's me," Peter said into her ear, his arms still around her waist. His voice was tense, as if he spoke through clenched teeth. "When did you learn to get out of handcuffs?"

"A couple of minutes ago," Kate said.

"You're going to be the death of me."

"But probably not today," Kate said. "Today we have to help Logan."

"Getting yourself shot would not be helpful."

"Then let's do something else." Kate struggled against Peter's grip, and he let her go.

"Fine," he said. "But I lead and you don't talk. You follow directions. Got it?"

Kate nodded eagerly before he could change his mind. He took her by the hand and led her around the trailer, keeping in the brush until they reached the back. Then he crept close enough to peer into a window while still gripping Kate's hand. Kate stood on tiptoes to peek through the window beside him. He glared at her but didn't say anything.

The inside of the trailer was half slum dwelling and half laboratory, though even the lab half seemed to be created from cast-offs. Kate gasped softly as she realized this was the meth lab the Rangers were looking for. *These could be the people who took Vanessa!* Peter squeezed her hand and gave her a warning look.

Four young people stood among the crowded mess that was the trailer. A thin kid with bad skin stood close to Logan, pointing a gun at the young actor's chest. The thin kid's head jerked back and forth between Logan and the hulking teenager who was bellowing at the girl and waving another gun in the air.

"Who told you to lead tours of my lab?" the boy yelled. "This ain't a game, Megan. You can't drag every guy you like over here like this is some kind of tourist trap!"

The girl pouted and crossed her arms over her chest. "I didn't think you'd be here, Zack. I wanted to be alone with him, and he wanted to see the place where David got his weed."

The hulking teen screeched in frustration. "I only sold that guy weed because you insisted on bringing *him* here too. And look how that turned out!" He paced in the small space. "What am I supposed to do now?" He turned to look sharply at her. "You're going to get us all killed! You know that?"

Megan smirked. "I'm not afraid of *them*. You're a big baby."

Zack pointed his gun at her. "If you weren't my cousin, *bang!* I'd take care of you right now!"

She didn't even flinch. "I'm not afraid of *you*, either."

Kate put her lips close to Peter's ear. "We have to get Logan out of there."

Peter shook his head. "We wait for Sam."

"We got to do something, Zack," the thinner teenager said. "This guy was asking Lucky questions and now Megan too."

That was when Kate recognized the boy. He was one of the two guys who'd held Logan in the parking lot of the motel. The skinny kid was the one who ran away.

"I don't need to hear from you either, Rat," Zack said, pointing his gun at the thinner boy, though it looked more like he was gesturing than threatening. "I need to think."

"Sure," Megan said. "Because you're good at that."

The tension inside the small trailer was so thick that Kate could almost feel the pressure of it from where she stood. She suspected Zack wouldn't be pushed much further before he blew.

"Maybe we should call the boss," Rat said.

Zack had paced away from him a few steps, but he whirled around at that suggestion. "No. We can't tell the boss."

"You aren't scared, are you?" Megan taunted.

"You would be too if you weren't stupid."

Kate leaned close to Peter again. "Why doesn't Logan say anything?"

"Because he's smart enough not to draw attention to himself. Right now, they're concentrating on one another."

That made sense, but Kate doubted she could have stood so still and quiet with guns being waved around. Then, as if Kate's questions had jinxed the situation, Zack turned his fierce anger toward Logan. "Who knows you're here?"

"Lots of people," Logan said. "I don't follow directions on some note without making sure people know where I am."

Zack turned to look at his cousin. "You gave him a note?"

"No, I gave it to his *mom*," Megan said. "He was hanging out with her at the Pizza Shack."

Zack turned back to Logan. "Where is she?"

"With her boyfriend," Logan said. "The homicide detective."

Zack groaned. "Where's the note?"

"Out in the car," Megan said. "I saw it."

"Go get it," Zack told her.

She crossed her arms over her chest again. "I'm not your servant." He pointed the gun at her, and she laughed. "Sure, shoot me. Dad will kill you."

Zack groaned again. He waved his gun at Rat. "Go find the note in the car."

Rat turned a sullen glare toward Megan and headed for the door, shoving his gun into the waistband at the back of his pants as he walked.

"I need to keep that kid from going back inside," Peter said. Staying low, he trotted around the end of the Airstream with Kate directly behind him. At the side of the trailer, they peeked around the corner, and Kate gasped again. Rat had his hands on his head and was being hustled away from the trailer by a Texas Ranger.

Peter leaned around the corner and waved at Sam, who was standing next to the door of the Airstream. The Ranger nodded but waved for Peter to stay back. Peter turned around and trotted back to the spot next to the window.

"Hurry up, Rat!" Zack shouted from his spot near Logan. The big teenager held his gun steady on the young actor, but Logan showed no sign of being worried.

"Maybe he decided to cut out on you," Logan said quietly.

"Shut up," Zack said. "He wouldn't do that. He's probably having trouble finding the note." He risked a fast glance at Megan. "You should have gotten it."

"It wasn't hidden," Megan said scornfully. "Rat's an idiot."

"Then you go get it."

Megan huffed. "Fine. But don't hurt him while I'm gone. I like him. He's cute."

Again, Peter and Kate ran around the end of the trailer to see what would happen when the girl walked out. As soon as she stepped outside, Sam held her at gunpoint. She treated the Ranger's gun with considerably more respect than she had her cousin's.

Sam said something to the girl, but Peter and Kate were too far away to hear. Her response was to smirk at him and turn toward the door. "You better come out here, Zack," she called. "Your friend Rat took off with Logan's car."

The door banged open, and Kate heard, "What are you—"

He never got to finish his sentence before he flew out of the doorway and hit the ground in front of the Airstream steps hard, knocking the gun from his hand.

Logan dashed out of the trailer as Zack scrambled for his gun, only to freeze when Sam shouted. Kate felt weak in the knees with relief as the Ranger cuffed Zack and his cousin. Logan was free, and no one had been shot. She was amazed.

She ran into the clearing then, jumping in front of Zack before Sam could haul him to a vehicle. "Where's my daughter?"

"Huh?"

Megan glared at Kate. "That's Logan's mom."

"No, I'm not. I'm Vanessa's mom. Where is she?"

"Who's Vanessa?" the tall teenager asked, his expression confused.

"She was part of the archaeology team at the river," Kate said. "The missing team. What did you do to them?"

"Lady, I don't know what you're talking about."

"You certainly do," Peter said. "You sold drugs to one of them. I heard you talking about selling weed to David."

"Sure, David," the kid said, then glared at his cousin. "Because she brought him here. But I didn't meet any girls."

"Then why is she missing?" Kate asked, launching herself at the tall teen and pulling on the front of his shirt. The boy shrank back, wide-eyed. Peter put his arms around Kate and guided her away.

"Kate, let Sam handle this," he said.

"But they know about Vanessa!" Kate wailed. "They have to tell me!"

"Hey, lady," Megan said, twisting as an officer was hauling her toward an SUV. "He really doesn't."

Kate pulled free from Peter and raced over to the girl as she and the officer reached the SUV. "Do you?" she asked.

The girl shook her head. "No, but you should probably ask—"

Her cousin bellowed at her to shut up before she got them all killed.

She glared at him. "I'm not scared." She leaned toward Kate. "Ask Shirley Thompson."

"Who's that?"

"The witch who runs the Pizza Shack," Megan said. "And this shack too. Oh, and you should ask her boyfriend."

"We're dead," Zack wailed. "We are so dead!" He kept it up until they shoved him into the backseat of one of the SUVs.

Peter never even looked at the wailing teenager. He kept his eyes on Megan. "Shirley Thompson has a boyfriend?"

"Yeah, hard to believe, huh?" Megan said. "But he's as much of a crab as she is."

"Who is it?" Peter asked.

Megan folded her arms over her chest. "Maybe I shouldn't be telling you all of this. I need to keep something as leverage."

"Leverage?" Peter said. But Megan didn't answer. She mimed zipping her lips closed before one of the Rangers put her into another SUV.

Kate looked at Peter in shock. "When we first got here, we were standing right in front of the woman who took Vanessa and didn't know it."

"We still don't know that Shirley Thompson took Vanessa," Peter said calmly.

"She was running a meth lab," Kate answered, her volume rising with each word. "And her brother just happened to find Kevin Hunter and just happened to let him bleed to death on the way to the hospital."

"I know you're upset," Sam said as he walked back to her. "But we're going to get to the bottom of this." He looked at Peter. "We need to pick up the Thompson woman and her brother for a chat."

Kate looked around the clearing. "What if Vanessa and the others are right here somewhere? We only have the farmer's word for where he found Kevin. What if it was here?"

Sam nodded and looked at Peter. "I'm calling in techs to go over the lab. But you know how to avoid contaminating a crime scene if you want to look over this area." He pointed at Kate. "But you stay out of the Airstream. I don't want lawyers latching onto information about amateurs traipsing around inside the lab." Before she could retort, Sam held up a finger and fished his phone out of his pants. "This should be about Kevin Hunter's autopsy."

He answered the call and put it on speakerphone. The medical examiner on the other end launched into a list of complaints about the state of the body before it reached him. "The body had been thoroughly washed, including the hair, and I don't like how neat the clothes were. We got a small bit of trace from the wound where the knife scraped against bone, but nothing helpful there. Other than that, all we found were a couple of dog hairs on the kid's jeans. Again, I suspect I'd have gotten more if the body hadn't been cleaned up."

"So the body was tampered with at the hospital," Sam said.

"Didn't I hear the coroner there worked in a mortuary?"

"That's right," Sam said.

"That probably explains it; those mortuary guys are wash-happy. He sure didn't do us any favors."

"You didn't learn anything else from the body?" Sam asked.

"Well, cause of death was the stab wound, like we thought. I found some traces of a couple of different embalming products, but that was probably transferred from the coroner."

"This case has suffered from lots of helpful amateurs," Sam complained. "Did you get the drug screen back?"

"Yeah, this guy is clean. No drugs, no alcohol. He's not even a smoker."

Sam thanked the man and ended the call. Kate frowned at him. "I hope you weren't including me on your list of well-meaning amateurs messing things up."

"You could have gotten yourself killed," Sam said. Then he turned to point at Logan, who was walking over to join them. "And you could have too."

"That's not fair," Kate snapped. "In fact, we seem to have solved your meth lab case. You're welcome."

"Yeah, I know. And that's the only thing weighing in on your side," Sam said. "Though I would still rather you and Logan had gone home and left the investigation to us. We'll find Vanessa."

"Eventually," Kate said. "I believe you'll find her eventually. But the sooner she's found, the more likely she is to be found unhurt. You need all the help you can get since we have the meth lab but we still don't have my daughter."

"Fine," Sam said. "Then in the spirit of helping, let's see what we can find."

Sixteen

When Kate watched Peter climb into the shabby trailer, she carried with her an almost magical hope that he'd find Vanessa tied up in the bathroom, or perhaps a trapdoor leading down to a hastily dug underground bunker where the whole team waited patiently for rescue. She was stunned by the wave of despair that washed over her when he finally walked down the steps, looking sadly into her eyes and shaking his head. A single sob snuck out before Kate clamped down on her emotions. She was not going to cry and give Sam more reason to think of her as a meddling amateur.

"I didn't find anything in there, but that doesn't mean the techs won't," Peter said. "And we're likely to get a lot more when we question the farmer and his sister."

"I hope so," Kate said softly.

"I'm going to get Kate out of here," Peter called to Sam. "We'll connect with you after we have a cup of coffee and decompress a little."

Sam nodded. "Take your time."

Logan jogged over when he saw Peter and Kate heading down the road to where Peter had left his truck. "Are you two heading back into town?" he asked.

"Yeah," Peter said. "Kate needs some downtime."

Logan looked at Kate and gave her a half smile. "Sorry about leaving you behind when Megan suggested going to the trailer. I didn't want to give her any reason to back out."

He turned sad eyes toward the trailer. "I really thought I had found Vanessa."

"I know," Kate said. "You did what you felt was right for Vanessa. I'm always good with that." Then she forced a smile and added, "Even if I did have to ride Megan's motorbike."

Logan's eyes widened. "That's how you got to the trailer?" She nodded, and he laughed. "You know, Vanessa always said you were gutsy, but I don't think I quite believed it. That motorbike looked like an engine fire waiting to happen."

"It did cough a little. Do you want to go into town with us?" Kate asked. She saw Peter's frown from the corner of her eye, but it wasn't right to leave Logan out in the woods. He'd risked his life to help Vanessa. Plus, he was the one who'd faced down armed gunmen.

Logan looked at Peter. "Is that all right with you?"

"Sure, if you want," Peter said, though his tone was less than welcoming.

Logan nodded. "Actually, I need to get back to my luxury suite at the motel. I'm going to pack up my stuff and try to find a rental at the real estate office. Last night I heard things gnawing in the walls of the motel, so I think I'd rather not spend another night there."

Peter's frown eased. "Be careful, whatever you do. You were a huge part of taking down a meth lab. There will be people who don't like that. And meth addicts aren't known for their measured responses."

"I hadn't thought of that," Kate said. "You shouldn't be off on your own. I think you should stay at the cabin with us."

"You do?" Logan and Peter said in unison.

Kate looked directly at Peter. "I couldn't stand it if anyone else disappeared."

Peter gave in immediately. "Of course." He smiled at

Logan. "You should get your stuff and then join us for coffee. I'll show you how to get out to the cabin."

"Thanks," Logan said. "But I already know. I was out there this morning, letting Kate know what I'd found out from friends of Vanessa. That's what put us onto the whole drug thing."

"I'll look forward to hearing all the details of that," Peter said.

"Sure," Logan said. "Well, I should go get my stuff. And I could pick up a sleeping bag if I need to."

Peter shook his head. "That won't be necessary. Both of the chairs near the fireplace fold out into single beds. You can have one. I get the sofa bed."

Logan grinned. "Sure, that sounds great."

"Fine. I'm taking Kate to find some coffee. You need to check with Sam before you leave the scene. He may need to get a witness statement."

"Sure, I'll see you guys." Logan turned back to the clearing and headed for Sam. Kate looked with envy at the spring in the young actor's step. She couldn't believe he still had so much energy after everything he had been through.

Elijahville didn't have any of the old familiar coffee chains, so they finally settled for Restaurant, the otherwise-unnamed diner. Kate didn't really care. She was suddenly incredibly tired, nearly exhausted. But when Peter suggested they head back to the cabin so she could rest, she straightened her spine and shook her head. "I'm not a Victorian damsel. I don't need to lie down every time I face adversity."

"My offer wasn't sexist," Peter said. "You've been through a lot."

"Not as much as Vanessa has," she replied. Then she realized his remark echoed something she'd thought back at the meth lab. "Logan was still bouncy after all he'd been through. I couldn't believe how calmly he faced those guns."

"I doubt he was calm," Peter said. "That young man is an excellent actor." He grinned at her. "I might have to watch one of his movies."

"We should watch the one that was filmed in Stony Point," Kate said. "You'd see a bunch of my friends. Vanessa has a copy of it on DVD, since she's in it too. Maybe we can watch it together."

"I'd like that," Peter said. He glanced sideways at Kate. "I won't suggest a rest again, but try not to push yourself too hard. It doesn't help Vanessa if you get sick."

"I don't know what does help Vanessa," Kate whispered. If Peter heard her, he didn't reply.

The parking lot of Restaurant was more than half-full, and Peter's pickup fit right in. When they got out of the truck, Kate asked, "Aren't you worried about someone knifing your tires again?"

Peter shook his head. "This place actually has a parking lot camera." He pointed up at it. "Last time, I chose my parking space unwisely. If someone plays tricks on my truck again, we'll have their photo."

They walked into the shadowy diner and looked around for a table. It was well past lunch and early for supper, but the place was still surprisingly busy. Peter led Kate to a corner booth where a young woman was wiping the table.

Kate slipped into the seat, sliding past a spot where the vinyl had been patched with duct tape. Peter asked her if she wanted something to eat along with the coffee, but she shook her head. He ordered two coffees. As soon as the waitress left, he reached across the table and took Kate's hand.

She stared down at his sun-darkened hand covering her own. There was such a contrast between them. His hands were rough, while hers were smooth. Though her life hadn't been exactly easy, she knew Peter had been through far worse. "I'm glad you're here," she said.

"Where else would I be?" he asked.

"Home," she said.

He squeezed her hand. "Kate, ever since you've moved to Fort Worth, I've only felt like I'm really home when I'm with you. Home isn't a location. It's wherever you are."

She looked up at him and studied the lines the sun had pressed into the skin around his eyes. He was a huge comfort to her, especially now with Vanessa missing. Without Peter, she would be utterly untethered. "She's been missing so long."

"Listen, Vanessa is bright and strong and brave, like her mother. Don't be giving up on her."

"Her mother isn't very brave right now," Kate whispered. "She's terrified."

"Bravery isn't about fear. It's about fearless action."

She nodded, though she was having trouble processing what he said. She did appreciate the pep talk. "I don't think that awful woman from the pizza place is going to be very helpful."

"Possibly not, but I suspect her brother is cut from a different cloth. He didn't seem like the kind of guy who'd hurt young women. At the very least, he might have a line on this mysterious boyfriend that Megan mentioned."

"Megan may have been making that up," Kate said. "She seems like someone who likes attention."

"I hope Mick Thompson will tell us," Peter said.

Kate looked directly at him. "I hope so. Can you look at a person and know if he's the kind of man who would hurt young women? Because anytime some awful thing happens, people on the news always talk about how surprised they are. How the person didn't seem like a killer."

"People will say anything once the camera is rolling."

The waitress came back with the coffeepot, and they held off talking until she had poured their cups full.

"I've rarely met anyone really dangerous who didn't feel 'off' in some way," Peter said. "People are taught to ignore that because it's not polite to think of someone as creepy. But ignoring that instinctive feeling toward predators gets a lot of people hurt."

"And you don't think Mick Thompson is a predator?"

Peter shook his head. "Do you?"

"No. He seemed sad and tired, but not cruel." She looked up at him. "But that doesn't mean he wouldn't cover up for his sister. She seemed like someone who could hurt people."

"She'll probably be a tough nut," Peter said. "But if the brother is a good man with a good conscience, I suspect he'll crack when confronted."

"I hope so."

Peter tapped the edge of Kate's coffee mug. "Drink up. You'll need the caffeine, because I might have an idea." He fumbled out his phone and quickly made a call. Kate realized immediately that he had called Sam.

"Have you gathered up Mick Thompson and his sister yet?" Peter asked. "Where are you doing the questioning?" He paused and nodded. "Has Thompson cracked yet?"

Kate squirmed in her seat, wishing Peter would put the cell on speaker so she could hear Sam too.

"Look," Peter said, "I have an idea, and I'm bringing Kate

over. Thompson responded to her earlier. I think he might talk for her."

Again Kate squirmed through the silence that followed.

"I know it's not procedure," Peter said. "But there are three young people missing, and we need to find them—now." Peter nodded as he listened to Sam's response. Then he ended the call and dropped the phone in his pocket. "We need to meet Sam at the police station."

When they walked into the station, the angry woman from the pizza place glared at them both from the tiny barred cell in the corner, but she didn't speak. Kate glared back until Peter gently tugged her along to the tiny interrogation room.

Mick Thompson sat slumped on a metal folding chair, his elbows on the table in front of him and his face in his hands. Kate walked in quietly and took the seat across from him. Peter leaned against the wall in the corner, keeping a sharp eye on the farmer. The older man didn't look up, and Kate wasn't sure what to say. Finally, she cleared her throat quietly.

Thompson looked up at her in surprise. "You're a cop?"

Kate shook her head. "I'm a mother. I need your help."

"The kids from the dig," he said, then shook his head. "I don't know where they are."

"What do you know?" Kate asked. "You seem like a good guy, not someone who wants to see kids die. Not someone who sells drugs."

His eyes flashed. "I do not sell drugs."

"Your sister does," Kate said softly.

Mick groaned and dropped his head back into his hands. "I didn't know it was anything as bad as meth. I thought it was a little bit of pot." He looked up, his face a portrait of misery.

"Could your sister have taken those young people?" Kate asked.

"I don't think so," he said. "But I don't know."

"How about her boyfriend?" she asked.

"Boyfriend?" Mick echoed.

"One of the young people from the lab said she had a boyfriend."

"No." Mick shook his head. "She did once, but those two hate each other now."

"Who was it?" Kate asked.

"Otis Shore. He owns a convenience store."

Kate exchanged quick looks with Peter. She turned back to the farmer and wondered what else she should ask. "Mr. Thompson," Kate said gently, "did you find Kevin where you said you did? Did you find him at your farm?"

He shook his head. "I didn't find him. Shirley—my sister—did. She called me at the farm and told me she needed me. She gave me directions to that trailer, but she didn't tell me what she needed. I didn't know about the boy until I got there."

"Where did she say he came from?" she asked.

"She said he staggered up to the door of the trailer and banged on it. When she saw him bleeding all over everything, she called me. She called me instead of taking that poor kid to the hospital. I drove as fast as I could, but I couldn't get him there fast enough." He broke down and sobbed. "If she'd taken him . . . if she'd taken him herself . . . "

Kate didn't know what to do. She glanced at Peter, but his face didn't give away any suggestions. She reached out and put her hand on the farmer's arm. "Do you think your sister could have grabbed those kids? Could she have stabbed that young man?"

He looked up at her and shook his head. "I asked her, and she swore she didn't have anything to do with their disappearance."

"She might have told you what she thought you wanted to hear," Kate suggested. "Imagine if she did grab them. Where would she keep them?"

"I don't know. The trailer was our dad's fishing shack. After our folks died, I didn't know why she wanted that dump of a trailer. I guess she was planning this even then. But the only other properties she owns are the Pizza Shack and a crappy double-wide over in the trailer park down on Mitchell Road." Kate turned to look at Peter.

Peter stepped closer. "I'll make sure Sam is having both of those searched, and I'll tell him to collect the convenience store owner." He turned to look hard at the farmer. "Is there anything else you can tell us?"

The older man shook his head. "I took that boy to the hospital even though I was afraid that it was too late. Shirley should never have pulled out that knife, but I don't think she meant to hurt him worse than he already was." He rubbed his face with one hand. "I lied for my sister, but I had nothing to do with those kids disappearing. I honestly don't think Shirley did either."

Peter folded his arms over his chest. "When we talked before, you said Kevin didn't tell you anything. Is that the truth? Did he say anything to you about who hurt him?"

The farmer shook his head. "Only what I told you before. He kept telling me to hurry. I think he knew his time was close."

Peter seemed to ponder that a bit, letting the silence in the room stretch. Then he changed directions. "Kevin Hunter and his group found a body not long before they all disappeared," Peter said. "Could your sister have anything to do with that?"

"No," Thompson snapped. "My sister isn't a killer."

"I'm not sure you know your sister as well as you think," Peter said.

"Shirley always wanted more than she could have," the farmer said. "Even when she was little. That's made her bitter and selfish, but I don't think it turned her into a kidnapper. And I definitely don't think my sister is a murderer."

"You know," Peter said, "the family is always surprised whenever I find a murderer."

When they finished at the police station, they met Logan's car on the road and together began the winding drive back to the cabin. Kate stared out the window, trying to hide her frustration. Sam had responded to the information from Mick Thompson by mobilizing a search team to check out the area around the meth lab for any sign of blood and another team to check out the double-wide. He'd also sent someone to pick up Otis Shore, only to find the man was not at his store. "But finding your daughter and her friends is our priority. We'll get a dog," Sam told Kate, "and we'll put him on Kevin's trail. We didn't find anything at the farm because he was never there, but we should find something at the lab."

Kate wanted to go with them. She wanted to be in on the search. She wanted to be there when they tracked Kevin's trail, but Sam refused. So, instead of heading for the next step in the investigation, they were heading to the cabin. Kate felt like a kid being put in time-out.

"Sam is just thinking about the case," Peter said. "The more he limits our involvement, the better it'll look when this comes to trial."

"I don't care anything about a trial. I care about finding Vanessa."

"And Sam cares about that too."

Kate sighed, letting the rush of breath end in a frustrated moan. "I feel like we're spinning our wheels."

"But we're not. We know that one of the missing team members was a drug user," Peter said.

"David," Kate said.

"He led us to Shirley Thompson's meth lab. And we know Kevin was at the lab as well. It's where Mick Thompson picked him up."

"But Mick Thompson doesn't think his sister is involved in the disappearances," Kate said.

"True. But as I told him, family is often surprised." Peter gave Kate a reassuring look. "Sam is doing the only thing we can do right now—search. If we can turn up something, maybe he can use it to get Shirley to talk. Or maybe Otis Shore will be helpful when Sam's people finally track him down."

"I hope so," Kate said. Then she looked at Peter. "That leaves us with a totally different question. We assumed the disappearance of the dig team was connected with the body they found. That would mean Shirley killed someone before this, but who?"

"Sam said he's looking into anyone in Shirley's life who might have disappeared," Peter said. "He'll let us know if he finds anything."

"He'll let us know," Kate grumbled. "That's getting to be a very old song." She settled down, and they passed the rest of the drive in silence.

When they parked in the clearing next to the cabin, Logan bounded out of his car and swung a duffel bag over one shoulder. "I really appreciate this!" he yelled in their direction.

"We're happy to have you stay here," Kate called back. She heard Peter mutter something beside her, but when she turned to look at him, he gave her an innocent smile.

Logan was the first one to reach the cabin door, and Peter said, "Hold on, the door is locked."

"No, it's not even closed," Logan answered, giving the door a little push. It swung open easily.

Peter turned to look at Kate, but she put up her hands. "I locked it when we left earlier, I promise."

They walked into the cabin and Kate gasped. The tidy little cabin was a mess.

"Looks like we've had company," Peter said. Logan's notepad from the motel lay on the kitchen floor, having been swept from the table. All the cabinet doors in the kitchen were open and much of the contents lay on the counters or on the floor. Peter's overnight bag had been upturned over the futon.

Then they all froze at the sound of a loud crash from the loft. The intruder was still in the cabin.

Seventeen

Peter held up a hand and whispered, "You two wait here." He climbed the steep steps with one hand on the gun in his holster. Kate held her breath as he disappeared at the top of the steps.

Instantly, they heard more crashing and scrabbling claws. Peter yelled, "Look out below!"

Kate scrambled away from the foot of the loft steps. In seconds, a masked face looked over the loft edge. Then the large raccoon raced down the steep steps, tumbling down the last few in his haste.

"Stay back, and I'll take a shot!" Peter yelled.

"No!" Kate screamed. "Don't shoot it!"

"It could be rabid!" Peter yelled back, but he didn't shoot.

The raccoon didn't act rabid. It raced for the cabin door, running past Logan and Kate as if they weren't there. As soon as it was outside, Kate slammed the door closed behind it.

Peter clattered down the stairs. "No one else up there. You'll need to see if anything is missing."

"How did a raccoon get in here?" Kate asked.

"They're pretty clever," Peter said. "Are you sure you closed the door tightly?"

"I did more than that," Kate answered. "I locked it."

Peter walked over and peered at the lock. "Yeah, it looks like someone went at this with a pick." He stood again and looked over the mess. "And then the raccoon took advantage of the open door." He gave Kate a smile. "And I'm afraid it took advantage of the snacks you had in your luggage too."

"Oh no." Kate climbed quickly up the steps to the loft. She heard Peter following. The intruder had strewn her things across the bed, and the raccoon had come along behind and ripped open the granola bars and chocolate she'd packed. Kate moaned as she looked at the chaos. The raccoon was a messy eater. Then she noticed Peter surveying the scene, and she realized her underwear was strewn across the bed in clear sight. She could feel the blush heating her face. "Uh, I'll look for anything missing." She reached for the closest bra, now smeared with chocolate as if the raccoon had used it to clean up after his snack.

Peter reached out and caught her hand. "Try to do it without touching anything," he said. "Sam will want his crime scene techs to look over it all."

At the thought of stRangers poking through her under-wear, Kate's face felt hotter still. "I suppose we have to."

"Guys!" Logan yelled from downstairs. "You'll really want to see this!"

Peter took the lead down the steps with Kate right behind him. Logan was standing in the doorway of the small bath-room. He pointed inside. Kate's makeup bag had been dumped into the sink. Using Kate's lipstick, someone had written on the mirror, "Stop or they die."

Kate began to shake as she looked at the smeary writing. "They're still alive. They must be, or this person wouldn't be threatening to kill them. Right?" She looked at Peter desperately. "Right?"

"Right," he said, but Kate had learned to read Peter well in the last couple of years. He wasn't telling the truth. They might be alive, but they might not. The intruder could be lying. "We won't stop looking. You know that."

"I know," Kate said. "We have to find Vanessa."

"And I think we start by finding this person," Peter said.

"The writer of that is left-handed," Logan said from where he stood beside Kate.

"How do you know that?" she asked.

"I was in this movie once where I was a detective," Logan said. When Peter groaned, Logan gave him a sheepish smile. "I know, I know, it was just a movie. But I did a lot of research for it, and the handwriting analysis stuck with me. When it slants left on an upright surface like that, it's because the person is left-handed."

"It isn't slanting much," Kate said.

"But it is slanting some." Peter clapped Logan on the back. "Good call." He thought for a moment. "The farmer is right-handed, but his sister is left."

"You noticed that?" Kate said, surprised.

"I notice everything."

"But they're both in custody," Kate reminded him. "How could they have broken in?"

"They're in custody now, but we don't know how long ago this was written on the glass."

"I don't know if she had time. We were here this morning, and then we saw Shirley Thompson at the Pizza Shack at lunchtime."

"And she saw you, I imagine," Peter said. "Which might have made her angry enough to come trash the place. She certainly wasn't at the meth lab when Logan was grabbed. Plus her boyfriend is still at large, and we don't know if he's left-handed." He pulled his phone out of his pocket and frowned at the screen. "I can't get a decent signal."

"Try sitting on the futon," Kate suggested. "That's where I got the best signal."

"I don't want to risk contaminating the evidence. I'll walk around outside until I can find one." He pointed at each of them. "Don't touch anything."

"Yes sir," Logan agreed.

Kate nodded but gave Peter a look that said she wasn't thrilled with his tone.

He grinned in return and kissed her cheek before heading outside.

Kate turned to stare at the message on the mirror. As terrifying as it was to see the threat to Vanessa, she hoped that they could use it somehow to help them find her. She tried to sort through all the people they'd met in town to see if she could remember any left-handers, but then she shook her head. She hadn't noticed.

"What's wrong?" Logan asked.

"I would make a terrible Sherlock Holmes," Kate said. "I've met so many people since we got to Elijahville, and I couldn't tell you if any of them are left-handed."

"Zack was," Logan said. "But the other kid wasn't."

"How do you know?"

Logan shrugged. "He held his gun in his left hand." He nodded toward the mirror. "But I don't think he did this. Until Megan invited me to the meth lab, he had no reason to do it. And after that, he had no chance to do it."

"That the only one?" Kate asked.

Logan shrugged. "I noticed Shirley Thompson was left-handed when we were at the Pizza Shack. She wrote phone orders with her left hand."

"I'm a terrible detective," Kate said.

"You've been a little distracted."

The bite of tires on the dirt-and-gravel road outside drew their attention. "Wow, Sam was quick," Kate said as they headed out the door. To her surprise, the vehicle pulling up outside wasn't the Ranger's dark SUV. Instead, it was the little blue Mini Cooper that Kate knew well.

Vivi threw open her door and hopped out.

Kate rushed over and hugged her friend. "I didn't know you were coming out here. How did you find me?"

"Oh, you think you're the only one with detective skills?" Vivi asked with a grin. Then she laughed. "Actually, you told me where you were going. Don't you remember? In case you and Peter were eaten by bears? By the look of it, you narrowly escaped an attack."

Kate looked down at her ruined pants. "Oh, this is nothing," Kate said. "I crashed a motorbike."

Vivi gasped. "I've been so worried. I kept telling myself I was being ridiculous, and now I'm really sorry I didn't get here sooner. I had some things I had to wrap up, and I took off as quickly as I could. I didn't even book a hotel."

"There aren't any hotels," Logan said. "And you *really* don't want to stay at the local motel."

"You'll stay here, of course," Kate said. "The bed in the loft is huge. We can share."

Peter walked up the rough road and stopped at the car. "Does Sam know you're here?"

"It'll be a surprise," Vivi said cheerfully.

Peter groaned. "He is going to be thrilled when he learns the sleepover is growing."

Kate noticed Vivi smiling at Logan. "Logan's been a lot of help since he got here," Kate said.

"Yeah," Peter said drily. "He risked Kate's life and nearly got himself killed earlier."

"He found the meth lab," Kate said, pointedly ignoring Peter. "And he noticed our intruder was left-handed."

"Intruder?" Vivi yelped. "Meth lab? I have so much catching up to do."

At that, they turned to the sound of more wheels on the rough road. This time it was Sam's SUV, followed by a smaller SUV that Kate remembered from the dig site. It belonged to one of the female crime scene techs.

Sam was first out of the vehicle. He zeroed in on Vivi. "When did you get here?"

"Don't get all gushy at the sight of me," she said, giving him a flirty smile. "You know how embarrassed I get."

"Although interfering in an investigation doesn't seem to embarrass you," Sam said as he quirked an eyebrow.

"I consider it helping," she said.

"This is no place for you," Sam said. "Things are heating up, and I don't want you in the line of fire."

"I appreciate that," Vivi said, her smile never wavering. "But as long as Vanessa is missing, I'm going to be here with Kate."

"Vivi, it's dangerous," Sam said.

"I gathered as much," Vivi said. "See? I'm already picking up clues."

They all turned at the bark of Peter's laughter. "Is this where you show me how you handle a stubborn woman who insists on running toward danger instead of away from it?" Peter asked Sam, who scowled in reply.

The crime scene tech had joined the group, and she looked from the Ranger to the detective and back. "Should I get started inside?" she asked.

"Fine, yeah," Sam said. Then he pointed at Vivi. "We'll talk about this later."

"I always enjoy our conversations," Vivi said cheerfully. "But if you think I'm heading back to Sage Hills and leaving my friend to go through this alone, you're very confused about my character."

"But she's not alone," Sam said with obvious exasperation. "By the time we're done, she's going to have everyone she knows here."

"That's not likely," Kate said mildly. "I've only got two other friends in Texas. Paige is busy running her yarn shop and Adam, my literary agent—well, I don't think he has time to come out either, though he might enjoy it."

Sam shook his head as he stomped into the cabin.

Peter put one arm around Kate and the other around Vivi. "I suggest you both wait outside while the tech is inside. Let them concentrate on the job, and let Sam cool off awhile."

"No problem," Kate said sweetly. "I know how important it is to let bossy lawmen calm down. We'll wait."

They leaned against the side of Vivi's car, and Kate launched into a recap of everything that had happened since she got to Elijahville. Vivi listened with only the occasional question or gasp. Finally Kate ran out of steam. "I think that's all."

"That sounds like plenty," Vivi said, counting things off on her fingers. "You've been shot at, Peter had his tires slashed, Logan's been beat up and held at gunpoint, and now you've been threatened. I'd be terrified."

"I think I'm too worried to be terrified," Kate said. Then she smiled wryly. "And weird as it is to say, I've been shot at before."

Vivi worried her lower lip between her teeth for a moment, then finally asked, "Do you think everything is connected to this meth lab?"

Kate shook her head. "I think Sam believes so, but I don't. Why shoot at us when we hadn't made the first step toward finding the meth lab? Plus, why come here and trash the cabin when the whole business with Logan was unfolding? No, I think we're missing something."

Logan had walked over as Kate made her list of reasons, and he stood with his hands shoved in his jeans pockets. "Those guys at the meth lab didn't act like people who'd already been involved with a murder. If they had been, it shouldn't have been so hard to decide to shoot me."

"Plus," Kate said, "why knife Kevin when clearly the meth lab was full of guns?"

"Maybe because shooting a gun in a meth lab would be stupid." This came from Sam, who had walked up to the group as Kate was speaking. "The ingredients used are highly volatile. You'd be amazed at how many labs we find because they blew up. Shooting a gun in a situation like that can trigger an explosion."

"To be honest," Logan said, "those guys in the lab didn't really seem that bright. I'm not sure they would think that clearly."

"Maybe not, but Shirley Thompson might," Sam said.

Kate gestured toward the cabin. "Have you found anything yet?"

"The place is full of fingerprints, not surprisingly. I'll need to get prints from you and Logan so we can exclude them. Peter's are on file since he's in law enforcement."

A few minutes later, the crime scene tech came out of the cabin and walked over to get Kate's fingerprints. Kate expected to end up with fingers smeared with ink, but the tech had her press her finger to the screen of her cellphone. "We're high-tech now," she said with a smile. "This way I can print you and put the prints right into the system for comparison to the prints I've found here."

"Did you find anything useful inside?" Kate asked.

The young woman smiled but shook her head. "I cannot comment on an ongoing investigation."

Kate closed her eyes and willed her nerves to settle. "All I want is to find my daughter."

"We want that too," the young woman said. "I've never seen Sam so emotional on a case. This matters to all of us."

"Thank you," Kate said. "Can we go back in yet?"

The young woman nodded. "I finished the photos and prints. With the scene contaminated by the raccoon, it's tough to be sure what damage was caused by the animal and what was caused by the intruder."

"Well, I'd imagine it wasn't the raccoon that left the note," Vivi said.

The tech gave her a cheerful smile. "No, I expect you're right."

"And I'm afraid I didn't notice if the raccoon was left-handed," Logan said as he joined the group. The tech turned to him and actually blushed when she asked Logan for his fingerprints. The handsome young actor certainly had an interesting effect on people.

Logan was friendly in the face of the tech's response, but Kate was glad to see he didn't preen in the attention. He seemed to take such admiration in stride, and Kate was reminded again how surprising it was that he was so down-to-earth.

Finally the tech was done, and she left soon after. Peter walked over to put an arm around Kate. "I'm going into town with Sam to take another run at Shirley Thompson. I think this was her. You should all be fine here. I'll be back as soon as I can."

"Maybe we should come," Kate said. "At least as far as town. None of us has had supper."

"Actually," Vivi said, "I brought some things. We could eat here."

"Maybe save Peter a plate," Sam said as he walked up to join them. "We might be late. I'll eat in town. I'm staying at the motel."

Vivi smiled sweetly at him. "I hear it's lovely."

Sam laughed. "About as lovely as you heard. Please, stay here and stay out of trouble."

"Kate and I never go looking for trouble," Vivi said. "We do look for answers."

"That tends to be the same thing," Sam said. "Please stay here."

Vivi shrugged. "Maybe."

Sam opened his mouth, but Peter clapped him on the back and led him toward his SUV. "You might as well give it up. She's just teasing you."

Kate stood with Vivi and Logan, watching as Sam and Peter drove off in separate vehicles. Then Logan hauled the big cooler of food from Vivi's tiny backseat, and Kate helped with Vivi's bags. Night was finally settling into the woods, and Kate knew it must be after eight. Her stomach growled with that realization.

Vivi giggled at the sound. "Supper's almost ready."

"After we clean up a little," Kate said.

They walked through the gloom toward the cabin. Inside, Logan had flipped on the light, and a warm glow spread from the open doorway. Kate picked up her pace to get inside before the light drew in bugs. Near the door, she spotted something lying on the ground. The light from the doorway had made the small metal object sparkle. She bent to pick it up, wiping dirt from the smooth metal surface.

It was a tiny four-leaf clover post earring, or maybe a pin.

Kate studied it. The bent post was thicker and sharper than the back of an earring. It was definitely a pin. Kate gasped as she realized that it must have belonged to the intruder. She'd found a clue.

Eighteen

Stepping inside the cabin and closing the door behind her, Kate studied the tiny clover in her hand. Something about it looked familiar. Had she seen Shirley Thompson wearing it?

"What's that?" Vivi asked.

"I found it outside, next to the door," Kate said. "I believe the intruder lost it."

"How did Sam and the tech miss it?" Vivi asked.

"It's small," Kate said. "And it was pushed into the dirt a little. I think someone stepped on it."

"Or it's been there for a long time," Logan said as he walked over to peer into Kate's hand.

"I don't think so," Kate said. "It's dirty and bent, but the metal isn't tarnished at all. And it looks familiar. You saw Shirley Thompson; was she wearing this?"

Logan shrugged. "I don't know. It doesn't look familiar to me." He closed his eyes, clearly trying to remember. Then he opened them. "Shirley Thompson wasn't wearing earrings at the Pizza Shack."

"I'm pretty sure it's not an earring," Kate said. "The shaft is bent, but it's still sharper than the post on an earring. I think it's a pin."

"And it wouldn't have to belong to a woman," Vivi said.

At her words, Kate felt the faintest tug of memory. But then it passed, leaving her frustrated.

"Maybe you should make a list of everyone you've seen here and then try picturing each one," Vivi said.

"We've met a lot of people," Kate said.

"Can we make the list while we eat?" Logan asked. "I'm starving."

Kate agreed. She looked at the mess in the kitchen as she slipped the pin carefully into her pocket. "Don't you think we should clean up first? I hate the idea of eating after a raccoon."

Logan moaned. "I might starve to death."

"You'll have to take the risk," Vivi said. "Because I don't want to eat after a raccoon either."

With hunger giving them extra incentive, they soon had the lower floor of the cabin set to rights. Kate felt funny about handling Peter's things as she stuffed them back into his overnight bag, but she didn't want to leave them strewn across the futon and the floor either.

Finally, the main room was done. "Do you think we should clean the bathroom mirror?" Kate asked. "I hate the idea of facing those words every time I have to go in there."

"Let the manly man take care of it," Logan said. He struck an over-the-top action hero pose and then strode across the room and threw open the bathroom door, making both Kate and Vivi laugh. Then he seemed to deflate. "Apparently one of your other action heroes beat me to it. The mirror's clean."

Kate peeked around the door. Sure enough, the mirror was clean and shiny, and Kate's things were back in her cosmetics bag. "Peter," she said, feeling a rush of warmth. "He must have known it would be hard for me to look at the threat."

"He's a pretty good guy," Vivi said.

Kate nodded. "I know."

"Hey, keep in mind that I tried to be the hero," Logan said.

Kate patted him on the back. "You've got a lot of competition for that role around here." She turned to look at the stairs up to the loft. She really would have liked to clean up before anyone else saw her food-smeared underclothes, but her stomach was growling in sync with Logan's.

He pressed a hand to his stomach. "Feed me, please."

"Definitely," Kate said.

Vivi had unpacked her cooler. The table was nearly covered with deviled eggs, a couple of different salads, and a tray of sliced meats, cheese, and olives. Kate picked up a roll from the basket and breathed in the scent. "Are these homemade?"

"I know I went a little overboard. But I wasn't sure what everyone would like, and I guess I had some time on my hands yesterday when I really wanted to rush out here."

"You get no complaints from me," Logan said as he pulled open a fluffy roll and stuffed it with meat and cheese.

"Nor from me," Kate said. "This looks fantastic."

For a while after that, conversation paused as the delicious food reminded them how hungry they were. Eventually, the feeding frenzy slowed. One by one, they leaned away from the table. Kate reached into her pocket and took out the tiny clover pin. She turned it over and over in her hands.

"Had any ideas of who might have worn it?" Vivi asked.

Kate shook her head. "But it's a four-leaf clover, so maybe someone wore it for luck." Then her face lit up.

Logan made the connection at the same moment. "You're thinking of the waitress, Lucky."

"It does seem like something she might like," Kate said.

Logan stared at the small clover. "I don't remember seeing it on her."

"She might not wear it all the time," Vivi said. "I have a bunch of pins. I don't wear them all at the same time."

Kate groaned then. "A bunch of pins. I can think of one other suspect. Megan carried a bag covered with all kinds of buttons and pins."

Logan nodded. "I remember. But when would she have been here? She was at the Pizza Shack when we were there, and then she was at the meth lab. So I don't know when she would have had the opportunity."

"Unless she trashed the cabin right after we left it," Kate said, "and then went to the Pizza Shack. That might be why we didn't see her inside. She only arrived as we were leaving."

"I suppose," Logan said. "So we have two possible suspects. How do we figure out which one it is?"

Kate sighed. "I imagine Megan is still in custody, so we're probably going to have to tell Sam what we know. Then he can question her."

"Maybe we should take it to him," Vivi said with a grin. "And maybe we could stop and ask some questions of your waitress friend along the way."

Kate grinned back at her. "Now that's a plan."

They quickly cleaned up the kitchen and headed out to Logan's car.

Despite it being late for a Monday-night suppertime in such a rural area, the parking lot of Restaurant was busy. "This seems to be *the* social spot," Kate said as Logan slipped the low-slung car into a spot far from the door.

"I hope Lucky is still at work," Logan said. "I don't know where she lives."

"Maybe you could charm her address from one of the other waitresses," Vivi said. "I bet you're good at that."

They headed into the diner, and Kate looked around the crowded room. She spotted several people who looked vaguely familiar, probably because she'd been there several times and it was clearly the social hub of the town. She did recognize two officers, though the uniforms helped make the connection. And she saw the young man from the camera shop. She happened to lock eyes with him, and he nodded and smiled.

Logan turned to Kate, pulling her attention away from the crowd. "I see Lucky. Let me have the pin. I'll go see what she knows."

When Kate went to drop the little pin into his hand, she was jostled from behind and it fell to the floor. Kate caught a glimpse of the back of someone in a suit as she bent down and retrieved the pin. She handed it to Logan. "Be careful," she said.

"Always," he promised, and then he hurried into the maze of tables.

Vivi nudged Kate with her shoulder. "Want to grab a seat? We could get dessert."

"You have room for dessert after all that supper?" Kate asked, surprised.

Vivi shrugged. "What can I say? I have a speedy metabolism."

"I'm sure you do," Kate said. "I have to go to the ladies' room. If you want to get a table, I'll join you as soon as I come out."

"Terrific."

Kate slipped through the tables with less speed than Logan but with as much intent. She wanted to be certain she was back by the time Logan had anything to report from his chat with Lucky.

The large diner was really too noisy for Kate's taste. Country music played from speakers in the walls. Conversations had to be held over the sound of the music, and so the room was a buzz of voices with the occasional accompaniment of scraping chairs and clinking dishes. All in all, Kate preferred the quiet of the cabin.

She felt a sense of relief when she started down the narrow hall that led to the restrooms and away from the noise. She'd nearly reached the ladies' room door when a voice behind her spoke. "Mrs. Stevens?"

Kate turned to face the coroner, Derek Hurley, who smiled nervously at her. "Dr. Hurley, may I help you?" She gestured vaguely toward the ladies' room door.

"I found something out about the young man who died . . . Kevin Hunter? Actually, someone at the hospital gave me something that they think might have belonged to him."

"You should give it to Ranger Tennyson right away," Kate said. "What is it?"

"A voice recorder," the coroner said. He shuffled his feet. "The thing is, the person who found it didn't exactly *find* it."

"I don't understand."

The coroner sighed, his face a mask of sadness and disappointment. "I'm afraid the young person stole it." He waved a hand vaguely. "You've seen this town. It's not exactly a land of high wages. This person is very young, and she swore to me that she's never stolen anything from a patient before. She felt terrible about it."

"And she told you because . . . ?"

"I am not exactly a normal part of the hospital staff. I suppose she thought I'd be less inclined to rat her out. Plus, I handled her grandmother's funeral. I guess she trusts me. Families do sometimes form bonds during such a trying time."

"I see. But I still don't know why you didn't give it to the Rangers."

The coroner pulled nervously at his tie. "I'd rather not be put in a position of getting the girl into trouble. If I gave the recorder to you, then you could give it to the Ranger or your detective friend. I would only ask that you not tell them where you got it."

Kate hesitated. She didn't want to miss out on a possible piece of evidence, but she wasn't sure she could make that kind of promise.

"The recorder had been used," the coroner said.

That got Kate's attention. "By Kevin?"

He nodded. "There are other voices on the recording as well. Female voices and male. They're whispering. I had trouble making it out, but I'm sure the Rangers have the means to improve the recording."

"I'm sure they do. You should give me the recorder. I can't promise not to tell where I got it. But you should still give it to me."

The man sighed. "Think about it. That's all I ask. Be certain you need to tell before you do so."

"I can promise that," Kate said. She held out her hand.

"I don't have it on me. It's in my car," the coroner said. "I didn't know I'd run into you here. I actually wasn't sure what I was going to do with it. I mean, I wanted to do the right thing, of course."

"Of course," Kate said.

A door to the parking lot faced the ladies' room door. It was solid wood with a crash bar. It had a sign warning that it was an emergency exit only and an alarm would sound if opened. The coroner ignored the sign and pushed the door open. "The alarm on this door hasn't worked in years. My car is right out here."

"I should let my friends know where I'm going," Kate said.

The coroner paused. "You're not going anywhere. I'm going to give you the recorder, and I'm leaving. If possible, I would prefer no one see me with you—in case you do decide to keep my confidence."

Kate looked out into the darkness and then turned her eyes back toward the diner. With so many attacks on them, maybe she shouldn't be out in a dark parking lot without letting someone know. But the coroner wasn't exactly a big, tough guy.

"I'm going to have to leave now," the coroner said, pulling at his tie again. "I'll think of some other way to get it into the proper hands, but if you tell your police friends that I have it, I'll deny it—vehemently."

Kate couldn't let the man leave. Vanessa's voice might be on the recorder along with clues that would finally help them find her. "Fine," she said. "I'll take it."

The man dropped his hand from his tie and smiled. "I'm glad. I'll be so glad to get rid of that thing."

As Kate followed him outside, she had a thought. The tie he'd been picking at was different from the one he'd worn at the hospital. That wasn't surprising. But the difference that suddenly lit up in her mind wasn't the fabric of the tie, but the lack of a tie pin.

She gasped softly as the realization hit her. His tie in the hospital had been held together with a tie pin. A tiny horseshoe. She remembered it clearly. And anyone who would wear a horseshoe for luck would probably wear a four-leaf clover. She stopped walking and took a step backward.

The coroner must have heard the change in her footsteps because he turned around, drew a gun from his pocket, and aimed it squarely at her heart.

Nineteen

The coroner looked at her with big, sad eyes. "What did I do to give myself away?"

"I remembered that you wore a tie pin," Kate said, careful to speak calmly despite the pounding of her heart in her chest. "You're not wearing one now because you lost it while searching the cabin today."

"You're a very clever woman," he said. "I'm going to have to insist that you come with me now."

"Or you'll shoot me in the parking lot?" Kate asked. "Wouldn't that draw a lot of attention?"

He laughed softly. "Maybe not as much as you'd think. It's noisy in there, and you'd be amazed at the abundance of gunfire around here. It's usually kids shooting cans."

"Is that a risk you're willing to take?" Kate asked.

"I won't have to." He took a step closer to her. "If you run, I'll catch you long before you reach the door. And if you scream, well, again, it's noisy in there. Either way, you *will* be coming with me."

"So you can kill me," she said. "The way you killed Kevin."

"I didn't kill that boy." He took a couple of deep breaths, then waved toward a parked car with the gun barrel. "That's my car. It's unlocked. Get in. You can drive. I'll direct."

"I want to see my daughter."

"That's the plan," he said. "Now get in."

Kate didn't think getting in a murderer's car was a good idea. She'd done it before, but she was beginning to suspect that she pushed her luck far too often. Still, if this man had Vanessa, then maybe that was where he was intending to take her. So she did as he said and walked to the car. Kate opened the door and started to get in.

"Hold on," the coroner said. "Hand me your purse."

"My purse?"

"It wouldn't do to let you keep your phone."

Kate handed over her purse and waited tensely for him to go through it. He'd find that her phone wasn't in the purse. It was in her pocket. To her relief, without a glance, he threw her purse into the open dumpster near the car.

"Now we can go. Get in." Kate slipped into the car. As the coroner walked around to the passenger door, she took her phone from her pocket and dropped it into the narrow space between her seat and the center console.

With the gun held low and pointed at her side, the coroner looked around the lot. "Time to go."

They were soon out of the parking lot and heading down the highway. They didn't go far before reaching the Elijahville Funeral Home. Night had fallen and the unlit funeral home seemed to squat in the dark, a shadow against the night sky. "No tricks, Mrs. Stevens," the coroner said. "I would hate to have to kill you."

"I don't think I'd enjoy it much either," Kate said. "In that spirit, could you please not point that at me as we stumble around in the dark?"

"Just do what you're told."

They climbed out of the car. With only the interior light shining on him, Derek Hurley and his gun looked even more menacing. He gestured with it toward a narrow sidewalk that skirted the building. "Follow the walk. We'll go in the back door. I want to chat a little before I take you for your family reunion."

Fear bit at Kate's insides. Could he have killed Vanessa and the others? Would she soon be joining her daughter in a shallow grave? She shuffled along the sidewalk, half-expecting the hot burn of a bullet in the back at any moment.

"A little faster, if you please."

"I can't see," Kate said. "This is the fastest I can go unless you have a flashlight."

She felt the poke of the gun barrel in her back. "Faster." She walked a little faster. When they reached the side of the squat building, Kate could barely see anything at all. Only the nudge of the barrel in her back kept her from sitting down in the dark and refusing to budge.

"Stop," Hurley said. He eased around her, bumping her with the gun barrel several times. Then she heard the rattle of keys. Should she make a run for it while his back was turned? Or should she stay and find out where Vanessa could be? Before she could decide, the door opened and dim light spilled out. "Inside."

She went in, weaving her fingers together so Hurley wouldn't see her shaking hands. He directed her to a large office with beautiful dark furniture. "This is a big difference from the last office I saw you in," she said.

"People like to be surrounded by comfort and nice things when they're handling the death of a loved one," he said as he gestured toward a leather chair. She sat down, expecting him to walk to the other side of the desk and take a seat. Instead, he perched on the edge of the desk. "I'm not a monster, Mrs. Stevens."

"You kidnapped my daughter," she said.

"But I didn't hurt her. I didn't hurt any of them." He stopped and shook his head. "Actually, I had to get physical with Kevin Hunter. He wanted to be everyone's hero."

"Until you stabbed him in the back."

"No." He pointed at her. "I did not stab that boy. He broke out of his container. We struggled, but he got the better of me. He ran away. I don't know who stabbed him."

"But you did kidnap them," she said.

"I did."

"Because you're involved with the meth lab somehow. That's who stabbed Kevin, wasn't it? Someone at the meth lab?"

"I don't know." His voice climbed. "I have never been involved with drugs. I could have been. I certainly needed the money, but I never did." He looked at her sharply. "Is that what the Rangers think—that there's a drug angle to all this?"

"A drug angle that will lead back to you," Kate said.

He shook his head. "No, it won't, because I was never involved with drugs. Gambling, on the other hand . . . that's an addiction I could tell you something about."

"Gambling?" Kate said. "You kidnapped the kids because of gambling?"

"Indirectly." He ran his hand over his bald head and then slumped slightly. "I didn't have a choice. Not after they dug up that body."

"You're not a drug pusher, but you hid a dead body in the woods?" she said. "Killing someone and burying them in the woods isn't really a step up from drugs."

"I didn't kill the man they dug up," Hurley said. "He *was* murdered, but I didn't do it. I only buried him."

"Why would you do that?" she said.

"I gamble, and I lose. That's why my wife left me. And I was going to lose this business, so I borrowed some money. I borrowed a lot of money. And I borrowed it from some very bad people. I thought I could make it back with a few wins."

"But you didn't," she said.

He shook his head. "The only way I could keep myself out of an unmarked grave of my own was to do a few jobs. I make bodies disappear. Normally, I put them into graves along with my regular clients. They keep each other company, you might say. But sometimes I don't have a client when the bodies show up. I can't store a murder victim here for very long. I have to do something with them."

"So you bury them in the woods," she said. "And their families never get closure, never find out what happened to them."

Hurley slammed his hand down on the desk. "I don't have a choice. And besides, the kind of people whacked by these bad guys, well, they're not very nice people either."

"They're people like you," Kate said.

"True enough. I'm not a very nice person," he admitted. "But I'm not a killer. I only work for killers."

"The body in the woods was a murder victim?"

He nodded. "Shot in the head. But not by me. I just stripped him, added a little lime, and buried him in the woods. The lime speeds up decomposition and makes it less likely some animal will dig up the remains. Unfortunately, animals weren't the only ones digging by the river."

"How did you know the kids had found the body?"

"I'd been keeping an eye on them," he said. "Driving out there every day."

"And you saw them discover your body dump."

He nodded. "I wasn't sure if it could be traced back to me, but it was bad no matter what. I'm supposed to make the bodies disappear for good."

"What did you intend to do with the young people you kidnapped?"

"Leave them where they are," he said. "They're safe enough there for now. I'm leaving town—I'm leaving the country. I've been putting together a little bit of money secretly. I knew this couldn't go on forever, but it's taken me awhile to get things in order. I'm going to be out of here and out of the country before the Rangers figure this out. All I have to do is tuck you away for a little while. That will throw enough of a monkey wrench into the investigation with emotions running hot and brains running slow. I'll be out of here while they're still looking for the drug dealer that grabbed you."

"Fine," Kate said. "Good plan. Now take me to Vanessa."

"Not yet," he said. "Unfortunately, I have one last thing I have to do here since I won't be coming back. A little shredding duty. So you're going to have to be put on ice for a little while."

"On ice?"

He smiled. "The cold room has the best lock. I promise you won't be in there long. I'll even loan you a blanket. Now get up." He pointed the gun sharply at her again.

Panic built in Kate as she tried to come up with a plan, something to stall. "So there was never a recording."

Hurley laughed. "Hardly." He looked Kate over. "I'd better search you. Your daughter was pretty tricky, smuggling her cellphone and trying to make a call. I caught her though." He gestured toward the wall of the office. "Step over there and lean against the wall."

Kate felt a wash of anger and shame as the stRanger checked her over for weapons. She was glad she'd left her phone in the car. When Hurley finished, he pushed her toward the office door. "Time to visit the cooler."

Kate stepped out into the hallway and stifled a gasp when she saw Logan standing there with a fire extinguisher over his head. She mouthed "gun" at him, then moved out of the way.

Logan swung the fire extinguisher at the coroner, slamming him in the shoulder. The gun flew from his hand, but Hurley recovered quickly. He punched Logan in the stomach as the actor raised the extinguisher for another swing. Logan doubled over. The older man drove the actor's face into his knee. Logan crumpled to the floor with his nose bleeding.

Kate shook off her shock and made a grab for the gun, but Hurley beat her to it. In the end, Kate and Logan were both kneeling on the floor, looking down the barrel of the gun.

"You people are becoming a serious nuisance," Hurley snarled. "Help the kid up, and you can both spend some time in the cold room."

Kate helped Logan to his feet, and Hurley brought the gun up close to Logan's face. "Who else is with you?"

"No one," Logan said, his voice thick from the nosebleed.

"Where's the little blonde I saw you two with at the diner?"

"Still at the diner. I saw you both in the hall and followed without telling her. There wasn't any time."

Hurley stared at Logan for a moment as if deciding whether to believe the young actor. Then he waved them down the hall with the gun.

Kate leaned close to Logan's ear. "Where's Vivi really?"

"Close," he said, covering the sound of the word with a cough.

"No talking, just walking," Hurley said. "Turn here."

They headed down another short hall and through a heavy door. Once inside, Hurley switched on a light. Inside was a workroom with bright lighting, unfamiliar instruments, examining tables, and an easy-to-clean tile floor.

Kate looked around and shivered. The air conditioning made the room considerably cooler than the hallway. Hurley saw her shiver. "Keeping this room cool helps with smells. I can't have any whiff of what death is really like seeping out of this room. But I'm afraid I have an even colder room for you two." He pointed with his gun toward a stainless steel door that looked like any walk-in freezer Kate had ever seen.

"If we freeze to death, you really will be a murderer," she said.

"It's not that much colder in there," he said. "I couldn't work on a body that was frozen solid. Now get in there."

"What about air?" Kate asked, still not moving. "There are two of us. What if we breathe up all the air?"

"It isn't airtight," Hurley said. "It vents to outside. Now I really must insist."

Kate took hold of the metal handle. The cold steel in her hand made her flinch. Then she hauled the door open. At that exact moment, the lights went out, plunging the room into complete darkness.

Kate felt a hand on her arm.

"Get down," Logan commanded.

Kate immediately dropped to her hands and knees. She still couldn't see anything, but she crawled quickly toward her best guess at where the door was. She must have wandered off course because she slammed into what felt like a metal cart, turning it over.

"Don't move!" Hurley yelled.

"Hurley." Logan's voice came from a totally different part of the room. "You can't get away with this."

Kate heard the hallway door swoosh open, the bottom of the door dragging slightly across the plush carpet. An emergency light from the end of the hall bathed Hurley in a soft red glow. Kate saw him point his gun at Logan.

"I'm tired of playing with you people," Hurley said.

The faint light also allowed Kate to see all the things that had tumbled off the table when she'd knocked it over. Her hand wrapped around a tub of something. It looked like a cold cream jar, but it felt heavier. She picked it up, raised herself up on her knees, and threw it as hard as she could.

When she was a little girl, her mom had insisted on teaching her how to throw a baseball. Now that certainly came in handy, as the heavy jar beaned Hurley in the head.

He dropped the gun and staggered slightly. Both Kate and Logan made a dash for the gun. Before they reached it, they heard a wild yell.

Vivi must have found the discarded fire extinguisher because that was what she used like a battering ram to mow Hurley down. The funeral director landed on the floor, skidding slightly on the slick tiles. Logan recovered the gun.

"Now," Kate said to the man sitting on the floor, "tell me where to find my daughter."

Before Hurley could answer, a line of armed men stormed down the hall, led by Sam and Peter. They quickly had Hurley in cuffs, and Peter had his arms around Kate. She pointed at Hurley. "He has Vanessa. Make him tell us where she is."

Hurley glared at her. If Peter hadn't held onto her, she might have launched herself right at Hurley to make him talk. "He has Vanessa!" she yelled. "We have to find her."

Sam walked over to Hurley and pulled a wallet from his jacket, opening it to his driver's license. He read out an address. "Is that where you're holding them?" he asked. "You might as well tell us. We're going to go look."

Hurley seemed to collapse then, his shoulders slumping. "They're fine. I didn't hurt them."

"Where is it?" Kate demanded. "I have to go. I have to go right now."

Sam started to say something, but Vivi slipped her arm through his. "We're going."

Sam nodded to her and called to one of his men. "Secure the scene and take Dr. Hurley down to the station. I'm taking this parade to Hurley's house."

Sandwiched between Peter and Logan in the backseat of the SUV, Kate barely resisted telling Sam to drive faster. Peter kept her distracted by asking her questions about what happened when Hurley had grabbed her.

"I can't believe you went outside with him," Peter said.

"I can," Sam said.

"Do you want to hear this, or do you want to scold me?" Kate asked.

"I want to do both," Peter said.

Kate suddenly realized that she was missing an important part of the puzzle. She turned to Logan. "How did you know where I was?"

"Lucky recognized the pin," he said. "Hurley was big on lucky charms. He even had her pick numbers for him sometimes because her name was Lucky."

"I called to let Sam know that you were missing," Vivi said. "We suspected Hurley. But we knew Sam couldn't break into a business without a warrant."

"But *we* could," Logan said. "We found his car at the funeral home, so I went in."

"Once Logan was inside, I called Sam again to tell him I was pretty sure there were prowlers at the funeral home."

"And I told her to stay outside," Sam growled.

"Which I ignored," Vivi said cheerfully. "And you know the rest."

Kate nodded. "I appreciate the rescue. Now all I can do is hope he was telling the truth about not hurting them. Can you drive a little faster?"

As it turned out, Hurley lived quite a way outside of town in a nice house in the woods. Since they had more than enough probable cause, Sam and Peter broke the front door down. As soon as they were in the house, they could hear shouts coming from downstairs.

In the basement, four large dog crates had been reinforced with heavy-gauge barbed wire and padlocks. "Mom!" Vanessa yelled from one of the cages. "Peter! Logan!" She burst into tears.

Sam and Peter soon had Vanessa, Maddie, and David out of the cages. Vanessa clung to both Kate and Logan, crying the whole time. Kate was crying as well. When she noticed Maddie standing nearby, weeping silently and looking both wobbly and alone, Kate pulled her into the hug.

Twenty

As she sat sipping early-morning coffee at her small kitchen table, Kate had never been so perfectly happy with life. She was home and so was Vanessa. Technically, so was Logan. He was at their home at least, having spent the last several nights on the sofa. He and Vanessa were reluctant to be apart after the horror of Vanessa's abduction. Though the ordeal had been traumatic, Vanessa and the others were in good physical health. Kate was grateful for that.

Sam had continued to put pressure on the Thompson siblings, but the real breakthrough came when the Rangers picked up Otis Shore. He had been selling drugs through the convenience store and admitted to damaging Peter's truck at Shirley's request.

Not long after Shore had broken, Zack fell apart as well. He admitted that Kevin had come out of the woods and pounded on the door of the trailer, not knowing it was a meth lab. He thought he had found help to rescue the other kids. Once he realized that he'd stumbled into a worse situation than the one he'd escaped, he tried to run. Shirley Thompson had thrown the knife that killed him, and then she called her brother to help her cover it up.

The more Kate thought about it, the more sure she was that Mick Thompson had been confused about Kevin's last words. Kevin had been saying "Hurley" instead of "Hurry" as he drove him to the hospital. The young man had never given up trying to save his friends.

Kate was pulled out of her daydream by the scuff of Vanessa's slippers. "You're up early," Kate said.

"I'm finally feeling almost normal," Vanessa said quietly. "Logan is still sleeping."

Kate nodded, not wanting to admit that she was keeping very sharp track of where Logan was since he was staying with them. He'd been a big help in finding Vanessa, but that didn't mean Kate was blind to the fact that he was clearly in love with her daughter. Then she sighed at that thought. *Meddling again,* she mentally scolded herself.

"Penny for your thoughts," Vanessa said as she sat down across from her mother.

Kate smiled. "That's an old-fashioned offer."

"I know. I got it from you."

Kate made a face at her. Then she turned serious. "I'm so sorry we fought at the beginning of summer."

"I know," Vanessa said. "You hate it when we fight. I do too."

"But I'm the one who forgot that you're an adult now."

Vanessa laughed. "And I'm the one who forgot to act like one. Really, Mom, there's plenty of blame to go around. I'm not mad anymore. And I'm not going to throw away my career dreams and run off with Logan."

"He'd like it if you did," Kate said.

"Logan and I are just friends," Vanessa said.

"Peter and I are too," Kate said.

Again Vanessa laughed. "Hardly. That man is crazy in love with you."

"I don't know if I'd go that far," Kate said. "But Logan doesn't think of you as just a friend. He'll accept that, but that's not what he feels."

"You're imagining things."

"You forget, I've spent some very stressful time with Logan lately. I think I have the advantage here. He loves you."

"If he did, he'd say so," Vanessa argued.

A deep voice spoke from the living room. "Unless he was afraid of losing you entirely." Logan stepped into the kitchen. His dark hair was a tousled mess on his head, and he needed a shave. He looked less like a teen idol and more like a normal, uncertain young man. "I do love you, Vanessa. I'm fine with never acting on that and being friends forever. I don't expect you to be anything you don't want to be, but your mom is right. I love you."

Vanessa's eyes swam with tears, and she hopped up from the table. "I'm not interested in leaving college."

"I don't want you to," he said.

"I intend to have my own career."

He looked a little googly-eyed as the reality of what was happening dawned on him. "I want you to have it."

She nodded. "Then I might as well let you know that I love you too." Then she threw her arms around his neck and kissed him.

Kate averted her eyes. The kissing definitely went on a bit longer than she was totally comfortable with. "I think you two should know that since we've had a declaration of love, Logan's not going to be sleeping here any longer."

"Mom," Vanessa complained as she blushed deeply.

"Vanessa," Kate responded, and then she laughed. "I'm sure he can stay with Vivi."

"Whatever you think is best," Logan said, though he kept an arm around Vanessa as he said it.

Kate couldn't help but feel happy for Vanessa when she saw the look of love on her face. Still, she was glad to escape the scene at the call of the front doorbell. "I'll get that," she said as she jumped up and hurried through the house.

When she opened the front door, Peter stood there, looking good in his jeans and pale blue T-shirt. He held out a phone. "Your phone. It's been cleared from evidence," he said.

"Oh, good. I thought I was going to have to buy a new one."

"You never did tell me why it was wedged between the driver's seat and the console of Hurley's car," Peter said as Kate stepped aside to let him in the house.

"I knew you'd be looking for me," Kate said. "I remembered you could track the phone, and that would lead you to Hurley. Also, I didn't have time to silence it, so I figured if it rang, he wouldn't be able to reach it down there."

"You've got a good head on your shoulders," he said as he leaned forward to give her a sweet peck on the lips.

Kate looked at him suspiciously. "That's all? No fresh lecture on getting in the car with Hurley? No telling me how easily I could have been killed?"

"Don't you already know those things?" Peter asked.

Kate nodded. "I didn't have a choice about getting in the car with the gun and all. I wasn't thinking clearly. I was so worried about Vanessa."

"I know." He reached out and gently traced the line of her jaw, making Kate's skin tingle. "How is she?"

"She's bounced back faster than I have, but Logan was a big part of that."

"You like Logan now?" Peter asked.

Kate rolled her eyes. "I've always *liked* Logan, but he's recently risked his life to save me and to save Vanessa. So I'm upgrading my appreciation of him. Plus, he's in love with my daughter, and it turns out she loves him too."

"Wow, that's a lot of change," Peter said.

"It's been quite a morning," Kate said.

Peter tilted his head slightly to look at her. "I barely recognize the skittish woman from Maine, trying to convince me she didn't kill someone."

"Oh?" she said. "And you miss her?"

He shook his head. "I was wild about that brown-eyed girl the second I saw her, and I haven't changed my opinion since."

Kate turned her gaze down to the floor for a moment and then looked back up at him. "I appreciate everything you did to help me get Vanessa back. I know I am not the easiest person to date. And I know it had to go against all your instincts to support me while we were looking for Vanessa instead of sending me home. That means a lot to me."

"Kate Stevens," Peter said, "I will always choose you over my instincts, over my job, over everything else. Always."

Kate's breath caught in her throat, and her cheeks felt like they might catch fire. She stared at him without speaking.

He smiled, but now it looked a little sad. "It's OK. I'm not pushing you to feel the same way. One thing I'm definitely learning with you is how to be a patient man. The best things in life are worth waiting for."

Kate swallowed the lump in her throat and smiled. "Vanessa's ordeal has made me reassess my life," she said. "I've come a long way from that insecure woman you first met. I've found success as a designer and author. I have finally put away the vestiges of a very bad marriage. I've learned what it means to be independent." She leaned into the strong, sensitive man who had come to be such an important part of her life. "Maybe it's all right for me now to risk being a bit dependent again." Kate looked deep into Peter's eyes. "I can't see any part of my future without you."

Then she tiptoed and kissed him.

For a long time.

Learn more about Annie's fiction books at

AnniesFiction.com

- Access your e-books
- Discover exciting new series
- Read sample chapters
- Watch video book trailers
- Share your feedback

We've designed the Annie's Fiction website especially for you!

Plus, manage your account online!

- Check your account status
- Make payments online
- Update your address

Visit us at AnniesFiction.com